From a young age, whatever I read or watched would churn inside my head all day long, only to bloom into nightmares of fantastic proportions in my sleep. Imagine this, reading Shikari Shambu was one of the inspirations for my nightmares! Think about it, what does Shikari Shambu do? He escapes hair-raising situations by the skin of his nose. A tiger, a leopard or a bear would come growling for Shambu and our man would take to his heels. In his bid to escape danger, he would set off a chain of events. This would of course mean the poor creature chasing him would get bonked in the head by a log of wood or a rumbling rock or end up with similarly sorry fate.

Perhaps the relief of watching Shambu escape also raised the possibility of... what if he hadn't escaped? There could have been so many ways things that could have gone horribly wrong! My nightmares would give these possibilities a twist and land me in a cage in a zoo... at night with scary, chattering monkeys, peering at me with glowing eyes. On other occasions, I might be taking a walk in the woods... of course at night, and I'd lose my way only to stray into a land where deadly tigers and lions roamed free. From there, my nightmare would take on shades of a thriller as I desperately dodged the fearsome beasts and tried to reach safety. Unfortunately, my nightly horrors didn't oblige me with any of the slapstick comedy we've come to expect from Shambu's adventures.

But did that stop me from enjoying a good Shikari Shambu story? Not in the least. I'd eagerly leaf through my *Tinkle* to read Shambu's latest misadventure, all brought to life in artist V. B. Halbe's endearing style. I remember chortling as I read the stories penned by writer Luis M. Fernandes, especially those instances when Shambu's peaceful dreams were interrupted by tigers strangely scolding him, quite like his wife, Shanti!

Decades have passed since Shambu first ran through the pages of *Tinkle*. It's a testament to his popularity that even the children of today enjoy his antics, sometimes prompted by nostalgic parents, older siblings or even grandparents. As you browse through Tinkle's Origins, we hope you pass on the joy your memories bring you.

Happy reading,
Rajani Thindiath
Editor-in-Chief, Tinkle

EDITOR-IN-CHIEF	:	RAJANI THINDIATH
GROUP ART DIRECTOR	:	SAVIO MASCARENHAS
EDITORIAL TEAM	:	SEAN D'MELLO, APARNA SUNDARESAN, RITU MAHIMKAR, AASHLINE ROSE AVARACHAN, JUBEL D'CRUZ, POOJA WAGHELA
HEAD OF CREATIVE SERVICES	:	KURIAKOSE SAJU VAISIAN
DESIGN TEAM	:	TARUN SOMANATHAN, KETAN TONDWALKAR
COVER DESIGN	:	AKSHAY KHADILKAR

© Amar Chitra Katha Pvt. Ltd., May 2019, Reprinted March 2020
ISBN 978-93-88243-68-1
Published by Amar Chitra Katha Pvt. Ltd., 7th Floor, AFL House, Lok Bharati Complex,
Marol Maroshi Road, Andheri (East), Mumbai – 400059, India
Tel: +91 22 4918 888 1/2
www.tinkle.in | www.amarchitrakatha.com
Printed in India

Get in touch with us:

✉ tinklemail@ack-media.com   ⊕ www.tinkleonline.com
🐦 @TinkleMagazine   ⊕ www.amarchitrakatha.com
f Tinkle Comics Studio   ⊕ www.tinkle.in
⊙ @tinklecomicsstudio

Amar Chitra Katha Pvt.Ltd, 7th floor, AFL House, Lok Bharati Complex, Marol Maroshi Road, Andheri (East), Mumbai 400059

INDEX

INDEX

GOPAL THE JESTER

Illustrations : M. Mohandas

Based on a story sent by Ramdas Kamat, Bombay.

ONE DAY RAJA KRISHNA CHANDRA WAS TALKING WITH HIS COURT JESTER, GOPAL AND SOME OTHER COURTIERS.

GOPAL IS VERY QUIET TODAY. LET'S GET HIM TO TALK.

ER... GOPAL...

YES, YOUR MAJESTY?

WHAT IS THE DIFFERENCE BETWEEN YOU AND AN ASS?

?

THE DIFFERENCE IS ABOUT TWO FEET, YOUR MAJESTY.

WHAT!

ARE YOU SAYING THAT I AM AN... ER... HARRUMPH... NEVER MIND!

AND FOR THE REST OF THE DAY THE KING TOO BECAME VERY QUIET.

See and smile

Kalia
THE CROW

Script:
LUIS

Illustrations .
PRADEEP SATHE

WHAT'S THAT, KALIA?

IT'S CALLED A BALLOON.

IT WAS FLOATING AROUND AND I CAUGHT IT.

ER...KALIA, TODAY IS CHAMATAKA'S BIRTHDAY.

IS IT?

YES...AND I WANT TO GIVE HIM A PRESENT. A BALLOON, OR SOMETHING OF THAT SORT.

OH!

HERE YOU ARE.

YOU ARE SO GENEROUS.

I'LL GO AND GIVE IT TO HIM STRAIGHTAWAY.

WHY DON'T YOU COME ALONG WITH ME?

ALL RIGHT.

9

THE BRAVE SPARROW

Illustrations: M. Mohandas

Based on a story sent by Mansoor Rizvi, Bombay

IN A TALL TREE, THERE ONCE LIVED A HAPPY SPARROW FAMILY. ONE DAY—

YOU STAY HERE WITH THE CHILDREN. I'LL GO AND BRING YOU SOME FOOD.

MR. SPARROW SOON RETURNED WITH A JUICY WORM IN HIS BEAK.

BUT MRS. SPARROW HAD VANISHED.

WHERE COULD SHE HAVE GONE?

HE FLEW TO MR. CROW'S NEST.

THE KING'S MEN HAVE TAKEN YOUR WIFE AWAY, MR. SPARROW.

I'LL FIGHT THE KING AND BRING MY WIFE BACK.

HE COLLECTED SOME STICKS···

···MADE A CART···

···FOUND TWO FROGS TO DRAW IT···

···AND SET OUT FOR THE KING'S PALACE.

MR. SPARROW REACHED THE KING'S PALACE IN THE EVENING.

GIVE ME BACK MY WIFE!

THE KING WAS FURIOUS.

LET MY ELEPHANTS DEAL WITH THIS RASCAL!

THE GUARDS THREW MR. SPARROW TO THE ELEPHANTS.

AS THEY CAME TOWARDS HIM—

ANT, ANT COME AND HELP ME.

THE ANT CAME OUT FROM BEHIND MR. SPARROW'S EAR...

...GOT INTO AN ELEPHANT'S EAR...

...AND BIT IT.

ONE BY ONE THE ANT BIT EACH ELEPHANT AND SOON THEY WERE ALL UNCONSCIOUS.

This Happened to Me...

My brother and I once went to a temple in Simla. We took off our shoes outside the temple and went in. When we came out one of my shoes was missing. We looked around and saw a monkey holding it. We tried to get the shoe back from him but he refused to part with it.

Then a banana vendor sitting nearby said, "Don't you know monkeys? Give him something else and he'll lose interest in your shoe. You could give him a couple of bananas, if you like." So we bought two bananas and threw them towards the monkey. Sure enough he dropped the shoe and pounced on the bananas. I heaved a sigh of relief.

It was only later, much later, that we learnt that the banana vendor and the monkey were in business together!

Sent by
Rishi Kwatra,
Karnal

THE JUNGLE SCHOOL

BY
LUIS M. FERNANDES
AND
PRADEEP SATHE

WHAT'S HAPPENING... IT'S BECOMING DARKER AND DARKER!

LOOK, CHAMATAKA! A DRAGON IS SWALLOWING THE SUN!

IT MIGHT COME TO EAT US AFTERWARDS.

THAT'S A LOT OF NONSENSE, DOOB DOOB.

NO ONE'S SWALLOWING THE SUN. IT'S BECOMING DARKER BECAUSE THE MOON IS GRADUALLY COMING BETWEEN THE SUN AND THE EARTH.

IT'S A SOLAR ECLIPSE. NOTHING TO BE AFRAID OF.

17

SO THE WHOLE EARTH WILL BECOME DARK, EH?

NOT THE WHOLE EARTH... ONLY A SMALL PART.

...AND WE'RE IN THAT SMALL PART... HEEHEEHEE.

I COULD CATCH A NUMBER OF ANIMALS IN THIS DARKNESS.

ER...HOW LONG WILL THE MOON STAY BETWEEN THE EARTH AND THE SUN?

NOT LONG. THE MOON TRAVELS VERY FAST.

SO IT'LL SOON GET OUT OF THE WAY. THE LONGEST A TOTAL SOLAR ECLIPSE CAN LAST IS 7 MINUTES 40 SECONDS.

THEN I'D BETTER GET TO WORK FAST.

SEE, IT'S BECOMING BRIGHTER ALREADY.

DRAT!

THE DRAGON HAS SPAT OUT THE SUN. NOW IT MIGHT COME FOR US...YIEEEEE!

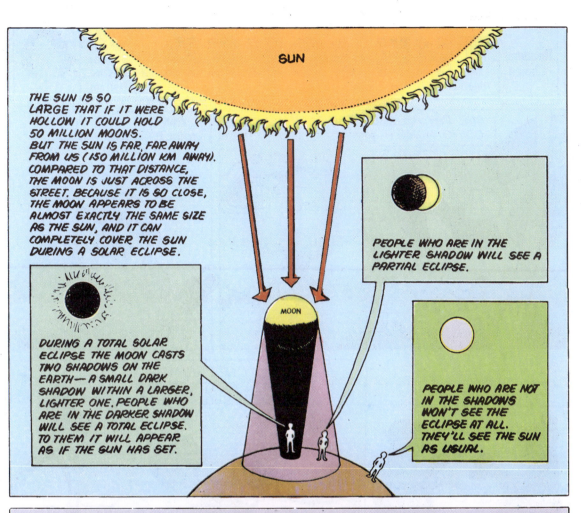

SUN

THE SUN IS SO LARGE THAT IF IT WERE HOLLOW IT COULD HOLD 50 MILLION MOONS. BUT THE SUN IS FAR, FAR AWAY FROM US (150 MILLION KM AWAY). COMPARED TO THAT DISTANCE, THE MOON IS JUST ACROSS THE STREET. BECAUSE IT IS SO CLOSE, THE MOON APPEARS TO BE ALMOST EXACTLY THE SAME SIZE AS THE SUN, AND IT CAN COMPLETELY COVER THE SUN DURING A SOLAR ECLIPSE.

MOON

DURING A TOTAL SOLAR ECLIPSE THE MOON CASTS TWO SHADOWS ON THE EARTH — A SMALL DARK SHADOW WITHIN A LARGER, LIGHTER ONE. PEOPLE WHO ARE IN THE DARKER SHADOW WILL SEE A TOTAL ECLIPSE. TO THEM IT WILL APPEAR AS IF THE SUN HAS SET.

PEOPLE WHO ARE IN THE LIGHTER SHADOW WILL SEE A PARTIAL ECLIPSE.

PEOPLE WHO ARE NOT IN THE SHADOWS WON'T SEE THE ECLIPSE AT ALL. THEY'LL SEE THE SUN AS USUAL.

THE OUTER ATMOSPHERE OF THE SUN, THE CORONA, CAN BE SEEN ONLY DURING A SOLAR ECLIPSE AND THAT TOO WHEN THE MOON COMPLETELY COVERS THE SUN.

CORONA

THE PROGRESS OF A TOTAL SOLAR ECLIPSE.

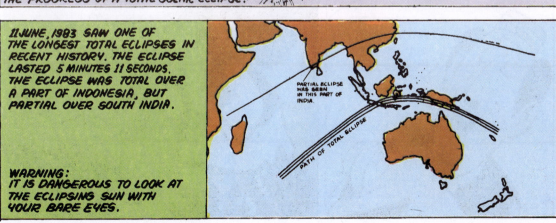

11 JUNE, 1983 SAW ONE OF THE LONGEST TOTAL ECLIPSES IN RECENT HISTORY. THE ECLIPSE LASTED 5 MINUTES 11 SECONDS. THE ECLIPSE WAS TOTAL OVER A PART OF INDONESIA, BUT PARTIAL OVER SOUTH INDIA.

WARNING: IT IS DANGEROUS TO LOOK AT THE ECLIPSING SUN WITH YOUR BARE EYES.

PARTIAL ECLIPSE WAS SEEN IN THIS PART OF INDIA.

PATH OF TOTAL ECLIPSE

Readers' Choice

THE JOKER

Illustrations : V. B. Halbe

a story sent by Shoma Dey, Ranchi

20

Illustrations :
Anand Mande

Based on an idea sent by
Virendra Kotecha, Kurseong

Mooshik

From an idea suggested by Rajesh T. Khilare, Aurangabad

To Our Readers*

TINKLE SUBSCRIPTIONS:

All new subscriptions and renewals of the old ones are accepted at:

PARTHA BOOKS DIVISION

Nav Prabhat Chambers, Ranade Road, Dadar, Bombay 400 028.

The annual subscription rate for 24 issues is Rs. 72/- per year (add Rs. 3/- on outstation cheques). Drafts/cheques/M.O. should be in favour of PARTHA BOOKS DIVISION.

All complaints pertaining to the old subscriptions (upto subscription No. 5000) should be addressed to India Book House Magazine Co, 249, D.N. Road, Bombay-400 001.

Readers' Contributions should be addressed to Editor, TINKLE, Mahalaxmi Chambers, (Basement), 22, Bhulabhai Desai Road, Bombay 400 026.

* Send a self-addressed stamped envelope if you want the story to be returned.
* Please do not send photographs until asked for.
* For "Readers' Choice" please send only folktales you have heard and not those you have read in books, magazines or textbooks. Rs. 25/- will be paid for every accepted contribution.

Mooshik :

Rs.10/- will be paid for every original idea accepted.

This Happened to Me :

You can write on your own strange, thrilling, or amusing experience or adventure. Rs. 15/- will be paid for every accepted contribution.

Reader's Mail :

1. Mail your letters to P. Bag No. 16541, Bombay 400 026.
2. Please give your address in your letters, if you want a reply.

TINKLE TRICKS AND TREATS

1. Mail your entry to Tinkle Competition Section, P. Bag No. 16541, Bombay 400 026.

2. With your entry you could send a self-addressed stamped (50 paise) envelope and collect 3 animal stickers.

3. The first 400 all-correct entries received by us will each win a copy of the AMAR INDIA WALL PAPER No. 14 dated June 1983.

Refer to the footnote under the Editor's Note

- CUT HERE -

TTT-30

ENTRY FORM*

NAME_____

_____

ADDRESS_____

_____

STATE_____

PIN ☐☐☐☐☐☐

MY SOLUTIONS:

A _____

_____

_____

_____

B _____

C _____

_____

_____

RAIN-MAKERS

Script:
Luis M. Fernandes

Illustrations :
Anand Mande

WHEN THE RAINS COME IN TIME, EVERYBODY IS HAPPY. BUT WHEN THEY DON'T, CROPS DRY UP AND THERE IS NO WATER TO DRINK. THEN PEOPLE GET WORRIED AND PRAY FOR RAIN OR SEND FOR THE RAIN-MAKERS.

THESE GENTLEMEN IN AMERICA, IN THE LAST CENTURY, THOUGHT THAT THEY COULD MAKE IT RAIN BY SHOOTING AT THE CLOUDS AND CREATING A LOT OF NOISE.

THEY DIDN'T SUCCEED.

IT IS SAID THAT THE GREAT TANSEN, WHO USED TO SING AT THE COURT OF EMPEROR AKBAR, COULD BRING DOWN RAIN BY SINGING THE RAGA, MEGH MALHAR.

MODERN RAIN-MAKERS GO UP IN AEROPLANES AND DROP PELLETS OF DRY ICE INTO THE CLOUDS. SOMETIMES, INSTEAD OF DROPPING DRY ICE, THEY RELEASE SMOKE GOT BY BURNING SILVER IODIDE. SOMETIMES SILVER IODIDE IS BURNT IN LARGE CONTAINERS ON THE GROUND ITSELF. DROPPING DRY ICE OR RELEASING SILVER IODIDE SMOKE INTO CLOUDS IS CALLED SEEDING.

SILVER IODIDE CRYSTALS

CLOUDS ARE MADE OF TINY DROPS OF WATER. THESE DROPS ARE TINIER THAN SPECKS OF DUST AND ARE TOO LIGHT TO FALL. IT IS BELIEVED THAT THE SILVER IODIDE OR THE BITS OF DRY ICE DROPPED INTO THE CLOUDS MAKE THE DROPS JOIN TOGETHER, SO THAT THEY BECOME BIGGER. WHEN THEY BECOME BIGGER THEY BECOME HEAVIER AND THEN THEY CAN FALL TO THE EARTH AS RAIN.

NO ONE CAN SAY IF SEEDING A CLOUD REALLY BRINGS ABOUT RAIN. IT IS ALMOST IMPOSSIBLE TO TELL WHETHER A CLOUD PRODUCED RAIN BECAUSE IT WAS SEEDED OR BECAUSE IT WAS ABOUT TO RAIN ANYWAY!

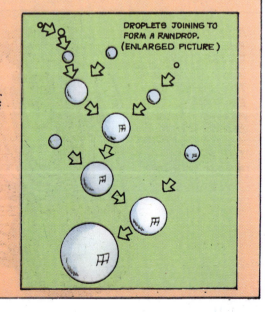

DROPLETS JOINING TO FORM A RAINDROP. (ENLARGED PICTURE)

EDITOR'S CHOICE

Yashesh Asher

My young friends,

Yashesh Asher of Bombay has sent us an amusing story.

There was a man who was an ardent admirer of the great Rajput, Rana Pratap, whose capital was at Chittorgarh.

One day, to his great joy, the man got an opportunity to play the part of Rana Pratap in a play his club was putting up.

On the great day, he put on the costume of the warrior and left for the concert hall.

People gaped at him but he did not even notice them. All he could think of was how he would portray Rana Pratap on the stage.

Absent-mindedly, he got on to a bus. The bus was crowded but unmindful of the people, he began to mumble his lines and rehearse his gestures.

At first the people were amused, but after some time they began to get fed up with him.

As the bus went on, our man began to gesture more vigorously and recite his lines more loudly and with greater emotion.

Soon he began to feel as if he were the Rana himself, and to everyone's horror pulled out his sword with a dramatic flourish.

At that moment the bus stopped for a moment and the conductor seizing the opportunity shouted, "Chittorgarh! Chittorgarh!"

"My capital!" gasped the man and pushing the other passengers aside, leapt out of the bus.

Affectionately yours,

Uncle Pai

Uncle Pai

Mooshik
From an idea suggested by Divya Vijayaraghavan, Nilgiris

(You don't have to draw the pictures when you send Mooshik ideas.)

Readers Write...

Every night I dream that I am in "TINKLE WORLD" and talking with Kalia, Chamataka, Doob-Doob and Babloo.
Vikas B. Naik
Bombay

Will Kalia ever have a wife ?
Or will he remain a bachelor all his life ?
Harish Dantale
56 A.P.O.

In the past whenever I saw boys flying kites, I was always puzzled about how kites fly and how they are made. I got my answer in TINKLE No. 26 and now I can make my own kites !
Pospendu Chaudhuri
Agartala

Your magazine is lovely, but I think the quality of paper is not so good. And since I love TINKLE very much I don't like it to be torn to pieces in a few days. So please do something about this.
Sukoon Banekia
Bombay

* Refer to the footnote under the Editor's Note

The Secret Reason

Illustrations: Ram Waeerkar

Based on a story sent by Deepa Sethi, Nainital

AS SOON AS THEY WERE FAR ENOUGH—

FOOL! IDIOT! FILLING YOUR STOMACH WITH WATER INSTEAD OF LADDOOS! I AM ASHAMED OF YOU!

BUT GURUJI...

...I HAD A REASON.

REASON? WHAT REASON?

JUST WATCH!

NOW, HASN'T THE MUD SETTLED PROPERLY BECAUSE OF THE WATER?

SO WHAT?

IN THE SAME WAY I WAS TRYING TO SETTLE THE LADDOOS IN MY STOMACH SO THAT I COULD EAT TO THE FULLEST.

. YOU WERE, WERE YOU?

YOU SELFISH WRETCH!

WHY DIDN'T YOU LET ME IN ON THE SECRET?

HOW THE HIPPOPOTAMUS LOST HIS FUR

Illustrations: M. Mohandas

Based on a story sent by Karsan D. Patel, Nairobi

LONG AGO THE HIPPOPOTAMUS HAD THICK AND SILKY FUR.

ONE DAY AS HE WAS STROLLING THROUGH A FOREST—

PLONK!

AAAAH! MY LEG HURTS. IT'S BROKEN!

THE HIPPOPOTAMUS PICKED HIMSELF UP AND LIMPED HOME.

LATER THAT DAY HIS FRIEND, MRS. RABBIT CAME TO VISIT HIM. AS SOON AS HE SAW HER HE LET OUT A LOUD MOAN.

OOOOOH!

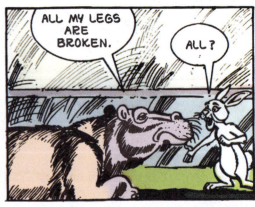

ONE DAY MRS. RABBIT CAME EARLIER THAN USUAL...

...AND WAS ASTONISHED TO SEE THE HIPPO, NOT ONLY ON HIS FEET, BUT DANCING!

WHAT A LIFE, WITHOUT A CARE!

TRA-LA-LA!

BROKEN LEGS INDEED!

WHAT A FOOL I'VE BEEN.

THAT NIGHT WHEN EVERYONE WAS ASLEEP, THE RABBIT CREPT UP TO THE HIPPO'S HOUSE AND SET IT ON FIRE.

FIRE!

FIRE!

FIRE!

The Selection Dance

Illustrations:
Anand Mande

Based on a story sent by S. Jnaneshwar, Secunderabad

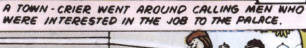

ONCE A KING CALLED HIS MINISTER.

I WISH TO APPOINT A NEW TAX COLLECTOR. AN HONEST MAN, MIND YOU!

YES, MAHARAJ.

A TOWN-CRIER WENT AROUND CALLING MEN WHO WERE INTERESTED IN THE JOB TO THE PALACE.

MANY MEN CAME.

PLEASE GO IN THROUGH THAT PASSAGE—ONE BY ONE. IT LEADS TO THE COURT.

WHEN THE FIRST MAN WENT IN—

ONE BY ONE ALL THE MEN WENT THROUGH THE PASSAGE AND WHEN THEY CAME OUT THE OTHER SIDE, THEY FOUND THEMSELVES IN THE KING'S PRESENCE.

FRIENDS, YOU HAVE TO PASS A TEST...

... A VERY SIMPLE TEST! YOU HAVE TO DANCE TO OUR MUSIC.

!?

WHAT A CRAZY TEST!

TRUST ME, MAHARAJ.

B...BUT DANCE! WE DON'T KNOW HOW TO DANCE.

IT DOES NOT MATTER, JUST SWAY, REVOLVE, JUMP, THUMP YOUR FEET— DO ANYTHING YOU WANT!

START!

NO. 37

TINKLE

THE FORTNIGHTLY FOR CHILDREN FROM THE HOUSE OF AMAR CHITRA KATHA

Rs. 3

THE CLEVER GOAT

EXPLORING THE SEAS

RANJHA AGAIN!

MEET THE PORTUGUESE MAN-OF-WAR

ALSO, KALIA AND OTHER REGULAR FEATURES

SAY HELLO TO

NIRA BENEGAL

Ms. Nira Benegal was a writer who worked with *Tinkle* during its early years. Initially Ms. Benegal was at the *India Book House* handling their *Echo* program that published illustrated storybooks for kids. Mr. Pai (Editor and co-founder of *Tinkle*), then, wanted Ms. Benegal to be a part of the newly established *Tinkle* comics.

When Ms. Benegal took on the role of an Associate Editor, she was responsible for proofreading the magazine pages before they went to press. She also checked for continuity and ensured that the panels transitioned smoothly within the stories. This, she says, felt like watching a film frame by frame.

The team Ms. Benegal worked with comprised of writers such as Mr. Subba Rao and Mr. Luis Fernandes. This was quite a close-knit group. Even though Ms. Benegal only worked half-days, she waited back to have lunch with her colleagues.

Ms. Benegal didn't just proofread stories but also scripted them occasionally. According to Ms. Benegal, each story was a team effort. Perhaps that's the secret behind those memorable stories.

Even today, Ms. Benegal believes that it's vital to be curious. She insists that we learn from all our experiences—good or bad. And above all, she urges the youth to have an immutable code of ethics. It's safe to say that just like her thoughts, her contribution to *Tinkle* has been exceptional.

THE MUSIC STARTED.

DANCE! EVERY ONE!

AND LET'S SEE WHAT FALLS OUT FROM YOUR CLOTHES.

STOP! I'VE SEEN ENOUGH!

MAHARAJ, HERE'S THE HONEST MAN YOU WANTED! HE'S THE ONLY ONE WHO DIDN'T TAKE ANYTHING FROM THE PASSAGE.

MEET THE Ladybird

Script : Ashvin

Illustrations : Pradeep Sathe

THERE ARE THOUSANDS OF SPECIES OF BEETLES. THE LADYBIRD, ALSO KNOWN AS LADYBUG OR LADY BEETLE, IS ONE SPECIES.

IT IS A TINY, GENTLE INSECT. BUT TAKE CARE NOT TO SQUASH IT. IT WILL GIVE OFF A STRONG UNPLEASANT SMELL.

SO BETTER WATCH THESE LADYBIRDS FROM A DISTANCE. THERE ARE SEVERAL VARIETIES. HERE ARE SOME OF THEM. MOST OF THEM ARE SPOTTED. SOME HAVE ONLY TWO SPOTS, OTHERS AS MANY AS TWENTY-TWO.

SOME LADYBIRDS HAVE STRIPES OR DIFFERENT PATTERNS OF DESIGNS.

THIS ONE HAS UNUSUAL MARKINGS THAT LOOK LIKE WRITING.

BEETLES ARE INSECTS, AND LIKE MOST OTHER INSECTS, THEY HAVE A PAIR OF A SPECIAL TYPE OF EYES, A PAIR OF FEELERS, THREE PAIRS OF LEGS AND TWO PAIRS OF WINGS.

LOOK! THIS ONE WANTS TO TAKE OFF AND HAS OPENED A PAIR OF HARD FRONT WINGS.

THERE IS A PAIR OF THIN, FLYING WINGS UNDER THE HARD WINGS AND IT IS WITH THESE WINGS THAT IT FLIES.

IT HAS LANDED NEAR A COLONY OF APHIDS — ITS FAVOURITE FOOD. THE APHIDS ARE HELPLESS BEFORE LADYBIRDS.

BUT DON'T PITY THE APHIDS. THEY DAMAGE CROPS, NOT ONLY BY FEEDING ON THE PLANTS, BUT ALSO BY TRANSMITTING PLANT DISEASES. SO LADYBIRDS DO US A GOOD TURN BY EATING THEM.

THE FEMALE LADYBIRD LAYS HER EGGS NEAR APHID COLONIES.

AFTER A WEEK, WHEN THE EGGS HATCH AND LARVAE COME OUT...

...THEY START FEEDING ON THE APHIDS. A SINGLE LARVA EATS FIFTY APHIDS A DAY.

THE LARVA GROWS FOR ABOUT THREE WEEKS...

...AND THEN IT STICKS ITS TAIL ONTO THE SURFACE OF A LEAF AND BECOMES A PUPA.

IN ONE WEEK THE ADULT LADYBIRD EMERGES FROM THE PUPA,...

...AND STARTS EATING APHIDS AGAIN.

THE LADYBIRDS THEMSELVES TASTE VERY BAD, SO INSECT-EATING BIRDS, LIKE THE GOLDEN ORIOLE, DON'T DARE EAT THEM. THE BRIGHT COLOURS OF LADYBIRDS IS A WARNING TO BIRDS TO KEEP OFF.

AT SUMMER'S END LARGE NUMBERS OF ADULT BEETLES FIND SHELTERED PLACES LIKE HOLLOW TREES OR EVEN BUILDINGS TO HIBERNATE FOR THE WINTER.

IN CALIFORNIA, U.S.A., AT THE END OF THE 19ᵀᴴ CENTURY, FRUIT ORCHARDS WERE ATTACKED BY SCALE INSECTS. FRUIT FARMERS RELEASED AN ARMY OF LITTLE LADYBIRDS WHICH GOBBLED UP THE FRUIT TREE INSECTS.

IT'S DIFFERENT! THERE ARE A FEW LADYBIRDS WHO ARE VEGETARIAN. THIS ONE FEEDS ON POTATO LEAVES.

SCALE INSECT

A LADYBIRD

THE TALKING LAMP

Based on a story sent by K. Binod Chandra Singh, Manipur

Illustrations: V. B. Halbe

"... SOMEBODY HELP ME!"

SHE SCREAMED AGAIN AND AGAIN...

HELP... HELP!

ENOUGH! ENOUGH!

COME OUT FROM THERE, YOU THIEF! WE'VE CAUGHT YOU AT LAST!

BH!!

ARE YOU ALL RIGHT? DO YOU WANT ANYONE TO STAY WITH YOU TONIGHT, GRANDMA?

NO.

I HAVE MY LAMPSTAND TO KEEP ME COMPANY.

BAH!

A FAKE COIN

Illustrations: V.B. Halbe

Based on a story sent by
S. Prasanna, Dhanbad

FORTY-FIVE...
FIFTY-FIVE...
SIXTY...
OH...

A COUNTERFEIT FIFTY PAISE COIN!

A CUSTOMER! I'LL PASS IT ON TO HIM.

CAN I HAVE LADOOS WORTH 50 PAISE.

OF COURSE.

HERE IS A RUPEE. PLEASE GIVE ME THE CHANGE.

HE RAISED THE FLAME IN THE LAMP...

LET ME LOOK AT MY SHINING NEW RUPEE.

OH GOD! A FAKE ONE RUPEE COIN! THE CHEAT!

THE LAZIEST OF ALL

Illustrations : Ram Waeerkar

Based on a story sent by Sumon Bhattacharjee, Shillong

A RICH MAN ONCE CAME UPON THREE MEN LAZING IN THE PARK.

HOW CAN YOU JUST LIE THERE AND WASTE YOUR TIME?

NONE OF THE THREE MEN ANSWERED.

OH! SO YOU ARE TOO LAZY TO EVEN ANSWER! TELL ME, WHO IS THE LAZIEST AMONG YOU?

I'LL GIVE FIVE RUPEES TO THE LAZIEST MAN.

I AM THE LAZIEST, GIVE ME THE PRIZE.

I'M LAZIER. GIVE ME THE MONEY.

PUT THE MONEY IN MY POCKET, WILL YOU.

THE RICH MAN LAUGHED AND PUT FIVE RUPEES IN HIS POCKET.

YOU CERTAINLY ARE THE LAZIEST MAN I HAVE EVER MET. HERE IS YOUR PRIZE.

KOKKAS AND HIS FLYING COT

Script: Meera Ugra   Illustrations: H.S. Chavan

Inspired by a tale from Vasudev Hindi, an ancient book
Story provided by : Smt. Shantidevi Motichandra

ONE DAY IN A KINGDOM LONG AGO—

WOODEN PIGEONS! FLYING!

GUARDS!

FOLLOW THOSE PIGEONS AND FIND OUT ALL ABOUT THEM!

LATER—

YOUR MAJESTY, THE PIGEONS HAVE BEEN MADE BY THE CARPENTER, KOKKAS. HE IS WAITING OUTSIDE.

BRING HIM IN.

SOON—

MARVELLOUS, KOKKAS! YOU ARE A GENIUS! BUT TELL ME...

...CAN YOU... ER... MAKE A BIGGER FLYING OBJECT?

I CAN, MY LORD!

THEN MAKE AN URANKHATOLA* FOR ME. I'LL REWARD YOU WELL.

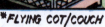
*FLYING COT/COUCH

KOKKAS LEFT THE COURT. A FEW WEEKS LATER, HE RETURNED—

THE FLYING COT IS READY, YOUR MAJESTY.

GOOD! LET'S SEE IT.

COME ON! LET'S FLY.

AHA! GREAT!

EVERYDAY AFTER THAT, KOKKAS TOOK THE KING FOR A JOY-RIDE. ONE DAY—

KOKKAS, THE QUEEN WANTS TO COME WITH US TODAY.

THE COT CAN TAKE THE WEIGHT OF ONLY TWO PERSONS. AND...

BUT THE KING INSISTED. THEREFORE—

ARE YOU ALL RIGHT?

Y...YES.

SOLDIERS! WE ARE IN ENEMY TERRITORY.

THE THREE PEOPLE WERE BROUGHT BEFORE THE KING.

WHEN THE KING LEARNT HOW THEY HAD COME TO HIS COUNTRY—

THROW THEM INTO PRISON!

DO YOU WANT TO JOIN THEM?

IN...P...PRISON?

YOU DON'T! JUST AS I THOUGHT! WELL, TEACH MY SONS YOUR CRAFT...

45

...AND YOU'LL BE A FREE MAN!

KOKKAS STARTED TO TEACH THE PRINCES.

SOME DAYS LATER HE BUILT A WOODEN HORSE.

I'LL SHOW YOU HOW TO FLY IT IN THE EVENING.

I'M GOING TO TAKE A NAP NOW.

AS KOKKAS SLEPT, ONE OF THE PRINCES BROUGHT THE HORSE OUT...

...MOUNTED IT AND TOOK OFF —

WHEEEEE!

THE NOISE WOKE UP KOKKAS. HE RUSHED OUT.

YOU FOOL!

WORKING FURIOUSLY, THE CARPENTER BUILT A FLYING WHEEL...

...AND HANGING ON TO IT...

...FLEW TO THE TOWER WHERE HIS KING AND QUEEN WERE KEPT.

QUICK, MAHARAJ! GRAB THE WHEEL!

HE'S TRYING TO RESCUE THE PRISONERS. SHOOT THEM DOWN!

WE'RE OUT OF RANGE OF THEIR ARROWS NOW.

STEERING AS BEST AS HE COULD, KOKKAS GUIDED THE FLYING WHEEL ACROSS THE ENEMY COUNTRY TO HIS OWN LAND.

WE'RE HOME!

The end

The Lion who Loved Dosas

Illustrations: M. Mohandas

Based on a story sent by Jones Paul, Bombay

GUNDAN AND GUNDI LIVED NEAR A JUNGLE.

EVERY DAY THEY WENT TO THE JUNGLE TO COLLECT FIREWOOD.

SUDDENLY, ONE DAY —

LOOK OUT, GUNDI!

EEEEE!

THEY TRIED TO HIDE BEHIND SOME BUSHES BUT THE LION SPOTTED THEM.

P...PLEASE... PLEASE DON'T KILL US!

GRRRR... I AM VERY HUNGRY. CAN YOU MAKE ME SOMETHING TO EAT?

OF COURSE! WE'LL COOK YOU ANYTHING YOU WANT.

CAN YOU MAKE DOSAS? I... (SLURP)...JUST LOVE DOSAS.

OF COURSE... ANYTHING!

GRRRR! BUT REMEMBER, I WILL BE AT YOUR HOUSE AT FIVE THIS EVENING. IF YOU DO NOT KEEP YOUR WORD, I WILL EAT YOU BOTH UP! GRRRRR!

THAT EVENING ...

MMM ... THAT SMELLS YUMMY!

HERE LET ME TASTE JUST A PIECE!

THE DOSA TASTED SO GOOD THAT—

GUNDAN! YOU ... YOU'VE EATEN UP THE WHOLE DOSA ...!

WHY DON'T YOU TASTE A PIECE, TOO?

GUNDAN AND GUNDI FORGOT ALL ABOUT THE LION ...

... UNTIL THE CLOCK REMINDED THEM.

TONG TONG TONG TONG TONG TONG

FIVE O'CLOCK! THE LION! NOW THERE ARE NO DOSAS LEFT ... HE'LL EAT US! WAAAH!

DON'T CRY, GUNDI! I HAVE AN IDEA. LISTEN ...

50

WHEN THE HUNGRY LION ARRIVED FOR HIS TREAT, HE SAW NO SIGN OF THE CHILDREN.

WHERE ARE THE CHILDREN? BUT I CAN SMELL THE OIL OF THE DOSAS... I CAN HARDLY WAIT TO TASTE THEM...!

THE LION WAS IN FOR A SURPRISE.

YEOWWW! WHAT A SLIPPERY FLOOR!

THE OIL HE HAD SMELT WAS ALL ON THE FLOOR, WHERE GUNDAN AND GUNDI HAD POURED IT.

IT WAS SO SLIPPERY THAT THE LION SKIDDED ALL THE WAY INTO THE NEXT ROOM.

I CAN SMELL THE RICH, SPICY AROMA OF CHUTNEY, AAA... AAAAH...

...CHOO! AAACHOO!

IT WAS NOT THE CHUTNEY HE HAD SMELT, BUT THE SPICES THAT GUNDAN AND GUNDI HAD SCATTERED ALL OVER THE FLOOR.

GRRR... WHERE ARE THOSE DEVILS? HOW DARE THEY PLAY TRICKS ON ME!

HE STORMED OUT IN A RAGE.

WHY, THERE THEY ARE— LAUGHING AT ME!

I SHALL...I SHALL SHAKE THE TREE UNTIL THEY FALL OFF! THEN I SHALL EAT THEM UP.

BUT THE CHILDREN WERE TOO CLEVER FOR THE LION ONCE AGAIN.

QUICK, GUNDI!

DOWN CAME A HEAP OF COCONUTS...

... WHICH KNOCKED THE WICKED LION FLAT!

YAY!

WHEN HE RECOVERED, THE POOR LION RAN AWAY WITHOUT A BACKWARD LOOK.

AND THE TWO CHILDREN NEVER SAW HIM AGAIN.

MEET THE GIRAFFE

Script: Ashvin

Illustrations: Pradeep Sathe

IN A SEMI-DESERT REGION OF AFRICA, A FEMALE GIRAFFE HAS GIVEN BIRTH TO A CALF. THE CALF STARTS WALKING WITHIN AN HOUR OF BIRTH. THE NEW-BORN WEIGHS 59 KG AND IS 2 M TALL.

NOTHING EXTRAORDINARY WHEN ONE'S MOTHER IS 5 M TALL!

HERE IS THE MOTHER SUCKLING HER CALF.

SHE HAD COME AWAY FROM HER HERD JUST TO DELIVER THE CALF. NOW SHE IS GOING BACK TO IT WITH HER YOUNG ONE. SHE LOOKS CAREFULLY HERE AND THERE...

SHE CAN SEE A GREAT WAY OFF BECAUSE OF HER HEIGHT, AND SHE HAS KEEN EYESIGHT TOO.

OH-OH... TWO LIONESSES ARE WAITING TO POUNCE ON HER CALF...!

IF SHE WERE ALONE SHE WOULD HAVE FLED, BUT THE BABY CAN'T RUN TOO FAST...

53

AS ONE OF THE LIONESSES APPROACHES, MOTHER GIRAFFE LASHES OUT POWERFULLY WITH HER HIND FOOT.

THE LIONESS IS STUNNED BY THE BLOW.
HER COMPANION STEPS BACK IN ALARM.

THE MOTHER AND HER CALF QUIETLY JOIN THEIR HERD.

LOOK, THE MALES ARE TALLER THAN THE FEMALES. THEY'RE 5·5 M TALL.

A LONG NECK IS VERY USEFUL WHEN YOU WANT TO GET AT JUICY LEAVES ON THE TOPS OF TREES.

EVEN THE CALF CHOOSES A BUSH SUITAIBLE TO HIS HEIGHT AND STARTS NIBBLING.

BESIDES A LONG NECK, THE GIRAFFE ALSO HAS A LONG TONGUE WHICH IT CAN CURL ROUND TWIGS AND LEAVES AND PULL THEM OFF THE BRANCHES. IT CAN GRASP LEAVES WITH ITS UPPER LIP TOO.

DRINKING PRESENTS A PROBLEM THOUGH. THEY HAVE TO SPREAD
THEIR LEGS WIDE APART OR HALF-KNEEL TO REACH THE WATER. A LION
COULD EASILY POUNCE ON ONE OF THEM WHEN THEY ARE IN THIS
AWKWARD POSITION. SO ONE OF THE GIRAFFES KEEPS WATCH WHILE
THE OTHERS DRINK. FORTUNATELY FOR THE ANIMALS THEY CAN
DO WITHOUT WATER FOR A LONG TIME.

GIRAFFES RARELY
SLEEP AND WHEN
THEY DO, ONE OF
THEM KEEPS WATCH.

THE SENTINEL HAS
HEARD A SOUND...

HE AWAKES THE HERD AND THE GIRAFFES TAKE TO THEIR HEELS. THEY CAN
GALLOP FASTER THAN A HORSE WHEN NECESSARY.

GIRAFFES ARE GENTLE CREATURES. OCCASIONALLY TWO MAY FIGHT. WHEN THEY DO, THEY BANG THEIR LONG POWERFUL NECKS TOGETHER UNTIL ONE OF THEM IS KNOCKED SILLY.

WHY ARE THESE TWO MALES FIGHTING? PERHAPS OVER A FEMALE.

BUT MATING ONLY TAKES PLACE WHEN THE FEMALE WISHES IT TO.

SHE WALKS WITH A PECULIAR GAIT BEFORE A MALE...

AND SOON THEY CIRCLE ONE ANOTHER IN A COURTSHIP CEREMONY.

ABOUT 450 DAYS LATER THE FEMALE WILL DELIVER A CALF AND ADD ONE MORE MEMBER TO THE HERD.

DESPITE ITS LONG NECK, THE GIRAFFE HAS ONLY SEVEN BONES IN ITS NECK LIKE ALL OTHER MAMMALS, INCLUDING MAN.

BUT, OF COURSE, THE GIRAFFE'S BONES ARE MUCH LONGER.

BIRDS HAVE 11 TO 25 BONES IN THEIR NECK SO THEIR NECKS ARE MORE FLEXIBLE.

FOR A LONG TIME EVERYONE THOUGHT THAT GIRAFFES WERE MUTE. NOW IT IS KNOWN THAT THE YOUNG BLEAT AND THAT ADULTS MAKE GRUNTING NOISES.

TINKLE TRICKS & TREATS* TTT-31

A
Find the missing number in the sequence.

| 3 | 8 | 18 | ? | 78 |

B
Find the odd man out.

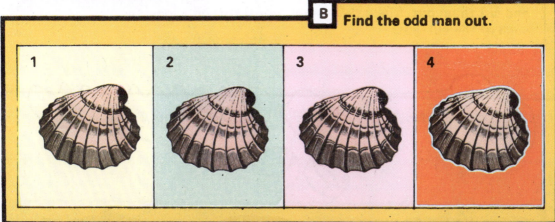

1   2   3   4

C
What is missing in the picture?

* Refer to the footnote under the Editor's Note

SOLUTIONS OF TTT-31

A.38. Every succeeding number is obtained by multiplying the previous number by 2 and then adding 2.

B. The third shell is different.

C. The shoelace on the left shoe is missing.

Fun with shadows

Ideas by Rajakaka

You will need : A table-lamp; a bare wall for a screen and your hands, of course!

Doob-Doob, the crocodile

Trace out these two shapes on a piece of stiff paper and cut them out. Make two paper loops. Attach a loop to each of the cut-outs.

Cut-out No. 1

Cut-out No. 2

Loops

Fix cut-out No. 1 on your index finger and cut-out No. 2 on your middle finger.

Hold out your hands and your fingers as shown in front of a lamp...

...and you'll see Doob-Doob's shadow on your wall.

Chamataka, the jackal

You don't need any cut-outs to see Chamataka's shadow. Only see that your fingers are in the right position

EDITOR'S CHOICE

Divya Jyoti

My young friends,

Kumar Divya Jyoti of Solan has sent us a Chinese tale which I wish to share with you.

One day a fisherman called Ah Chong set out in a small boat. After he reached a good spot he lowered his long line into the water and went away.

In the evening. Ah Chong returned and began to haul in the line, but it seemed unusually heavy. "I don't know if it is a fish," he thought, "but there is something very heavy!" When the hook came out he was astonished to find the links of a heavy gold chain. As he pulled, more and more links appeared. Soon the bottom of his boat was covered with shiny gold links. "I shall be wealthy. I will sell this chain and build a palace. I will be as rich as a king and have jewels and rich clothes and hundreds of servants."

Ah Chong hauled in more and more of the chain and soon the boat began to sink with the heavy weight. Ah Chong was a greedy man and he did not notice that the boat was sinking lower and lower. He could only see the glittering heap of gold.

Soon the boat sank to the bottom of the river and with great difficulty Ah Chong managed to swim ashore — without his boat, without any fish and without the gold chain!

Affectionately yours,

Anant Pai

Uncle Pai

59

Mooshik

From an idea suggested by Kedar Singh Arry, New Bombay

To Our Readers*

TINKLE SUBSCRIPTIONS:

All new subscriptions and renewals of the old ones are accepted at:

PARTHA BOOKS DIVISION

Nav Prabhat Chambers, Ranade Road, Dadar, Bombay 400 028.

The annual subscription rate for 24 issues is Rs. 72/- per year (add Rs. 3/- on outstation cheques) Drafts/cheques/M.O. should be in favour of PARTHA BOOKS DIVISION.

All complaints pertaining to the old subscriptions (upto subscription No. 5000) should be addressed to India Book House Magazine Co, 249, D.N. Road, Bombay-400 001.

Readers' Contributions should be addressed to Editor, TINKLE, Mahalaxmi Chambers, (Basement), 22, Bhulabhai Desai Road, Bombay 400 026.

* Send a self-addressed stamped envelope if you want the story to be returned.
* Please do not send photographs until asked for.
* For "Readers' Choice" please send only folk-tales you have heard and not those you have read in books, magazines or textbooks. Rs. 25/- will be paid for every accepted contribution.

Mooshik :
Rs.10/- will be paid for every original idea accepted.

This Happened to Me :
You can write on your own strange, thrilling, or amusing experience or adventure. Rs. 15/- will be paid for every accepted contribution.

Reader's Mail :
1. Mail your letters to: Tinkle P. Bag No. 16541, Bombay 400 026.
2. Please give your address in your letters, if you want a reply.

TINKLE TRICKS AND TREATS

1. Mail your entry to Tinkle Competition Section, P. Bag No. 16541, Bombay 400 026.
2. With your entry you could send a self-addressed stamped (50 paise) envelope and collect 3 animal stickers.
3. The first 400 all-correct entries received by us will each win a copy of the AMAR INDIA WALL PAPER No. 15 dated July 1983.

Refer to the footnote under the Editor's Note

---- CUT HERE ----

TTT-31

ENTRY FORM*

NAME _____

ADDRESS _____

_____

STATE _____

PIN ☐☐☐☐☐☐

MY SOLUTIONS:

A _____

_____

B _____

C _____

See and smile

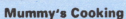

Readers Write...

Mummy's Cooking

Mummy, please do stop that cooking !
I can tell you without looking
It's going to be a waste,
Though I don't even know the taste.
So, Mummy, please do stop that cooking !

I've got a lot of work to do,
But after smelling your horrid stew,
My dislike for it is slowly growing
And on my face the strain is showing.
So, Mummy, please do stop that cooking !

Forget the stew, I now smell pie.
I shall be vomiting by and by.
Is this what we're having tonight ?
My future doesn't seem too bright.
So, Mummy, please do stop that cooking !

Talking of food, what about cake ?
It's easy to serve and easy to bake.
For another dish, what about custard ?
It's a million times better
Than your rice with mustard.

All the horrid things you make
Help me develop a whopping headache.
It sure keeps my nose at stake
And if I could, I'd jump in a lake.
So, Mummy, please do stop that cooking !

Shailaja and Arvind
Chandigarh

I would love to read about the porcupine,
the cheetah, the lion and the honey-bee.
So why don't you write about them ?

C. Ravikumar
Coimbatore

I am only 7 years old. I only see the pictures,
listen to the stories and enjoy the puzzles. But
my elder sisters take much more advantage
from TINKLE. Before they appear for any
General Knowledge exam, they refer to
TINKLE about inventions, discoveries and the
life histories of various animals.

S.R. Quadri
Nizamabad

I have been reading TINKLE regelarly I like it
very much. Kalia the crow is too clever for
the cunning Chamataka. But this serial is very
interesting

Jagdish Panyala
Visakhapatnam

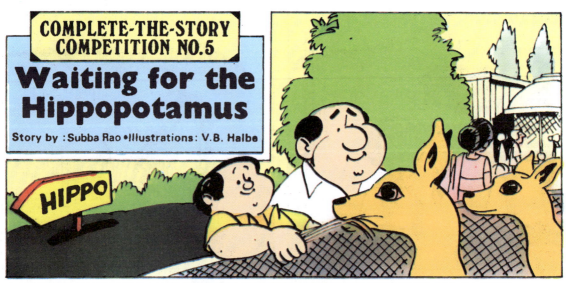

COMPLETE-THE-STORY COMPETITION NO.5

Waiting for the Hippopotamus

Story by : Subba Rao • Illustrations: V.B. Halbe

* Refer to the footnote under the Editor's Note

What Happens Next?*
Let your imagination wander
and see if you can develop
this story further in 500 words
or less.
There's a prize of Rs. 50/-
for the best entry but it
should reach us
before
30th June
1983.

SSSSSH! LISTEN

Illustrations: Anand Mande

HARES HAVE LARGE OUTER EARS.

HUMANS HAVE SMALLER OUTER EARS. WHATEVER THEIR SIZE, THE MAIN PURPOSE OF THE OUTER EARS IS TO GATHER SOUND AND FUNNEL IT ONTO THE EARDRUM.

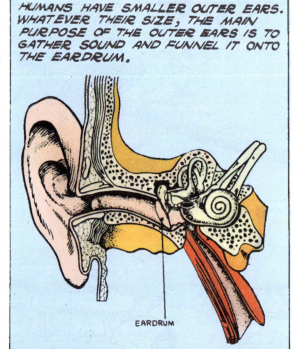

EARDRUM

THE EARDRUM IS A THIN PIECE OF TIGHTLY-STRETCHED SKIN AND IS CONNECTED TO THREE LITTLE BONES CALLED THE HAMMER, THE ANVIL AND THE STIRRUP.

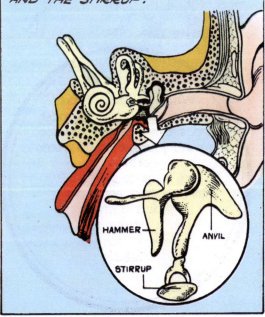

HAMMER   ANVIL

STIRRUP

ONE OF THE THREE LITTLE BONES, THE STIRRUP, IS IN TOUCH WITH THE INNER-MOST AND THE MOST IMPORTANT PART OF THE EAR—THE COCHLEA. THE COCHLEA MAY REMIND YOU OF A SNAIL. IT IS A TUBE COILED ROUND A CENTRAL CORE OF BONE. IT HAS THOUSANDS OF HAIR IN IT. THE FREE ENDS OF THE HAIR FLOAT IN A FLUID WITH WHICH THE TUBE IS FILLED.

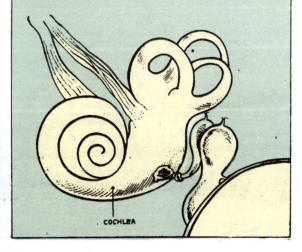

COCHLEA

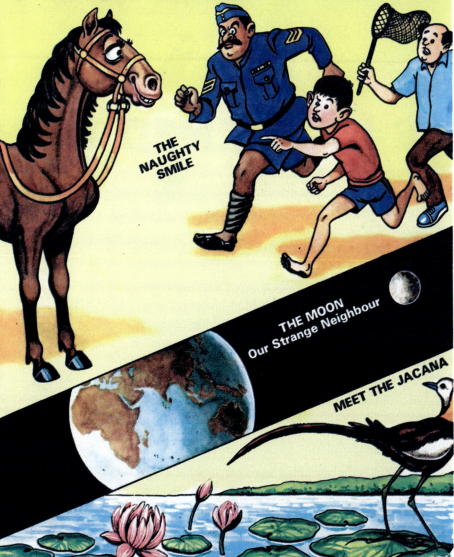

ABOUT
THIS HAPPENED TO ME

A good story can come from anywhere—from a nightmare, a daydream or even real life. A fight with your best friend, an encounter with an imaginary ghost or an embarrassing fall in public—This Happened to Me was started to celebrate these everyday stories and the people behind them.

Mr. Pai felt the popularity of *Reader's Digest* (a popular magazine of the time) was due to reader participation. The editors invited not only well-known editors to write but also encouraged 'non-writers' to send in short literary contributions. Mr. Subba Rao who was the ideas man for both *Amar Chitra Katha* and *Tinkle* suggested a reader contribution page in *Tinkle*, and that is how This Happened to Me came into being.

At the time, This Happened to Me made its debut readers were invited to send in their strange, thrilling or amusing adventures and experiences. Soon, hundreds of letters started pouring in every week. Each letter was read by a staff member. Though most were interesting, the volume of letters was so high that only the best of the best were passed along to the writer-editors. The writer-editors, in their turn, passed the letters they liked to Uncle Pai.

The entries selected by Uncle Pai were then proofread, cleaned up and illustrated. Not only did the winners get the joy of seeing their stories in print, but they also received a small cash prize. Till date, This Happened to Me, now known as It Happened to Me, remains one of *Tinkle*'s most loved and longest running features. The stories are sometimes exciting, sometimes wonky and sometimes scary but one thing remains constant, they always leave the reader with a smile.

THE THREE LITTLE BONES AND THE COCHLEA ARE RIGHT INSIDE THE HEAD. THEY'RE PROTECTED BY THE BONES OF THE SKULL AND SHUT OFF FROM THE OUTSIDE WORLD BY THE EARDRUM.

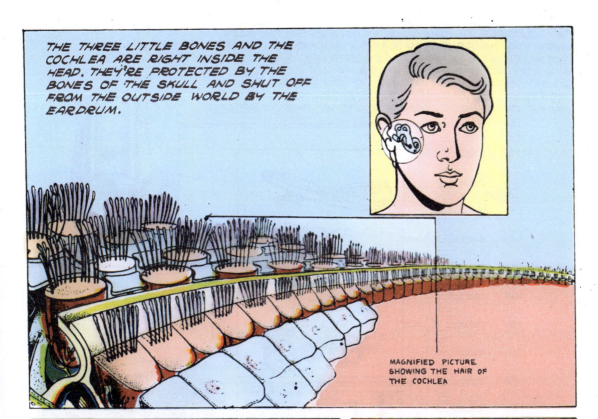

MAGNIFIED PICTURE SHOWING THE HAIR OF THE COCHLEA

IF THE EARDRUM IS HURT, THE WAY TO THE MIDDLE AND THE INNER PART OF THE EAR IS OPENED. THE EARDRUM CAN BE HURT BY BLOWS ON THE HEAD, BY SHARP OBJECTS AND EVEN LOUD SHARP NOISES.

HOW WE HEAR

WHEN A SOUND IS MADE, THE OUTER EAR COLLECTS IT AND SENDS IT ONTO THE EARDRUM. WHEN THE SOUND STRIKES THE EARDRUM, IT BEGINS TO MOVE TO AND FRO VERY FAST. THIS TO AND FRO MOVEMENT IS PASSED ONTO THE THREE TINY BONES AND THE LAST BONE OF THE GROUP PASSES IT ONTO THE FLUID IN THE COCHLEA. WHEN THE FLUID STARTS MOVING, THE HAIR IS DISTURBED AND IT SENDS SIGNALS TO THE BRAIN THROUGH A NERVE CALLED THE AUDITORY NERVE. THE BRAIN LETS US KNOW WHAT SOUND IS BEING MADE.

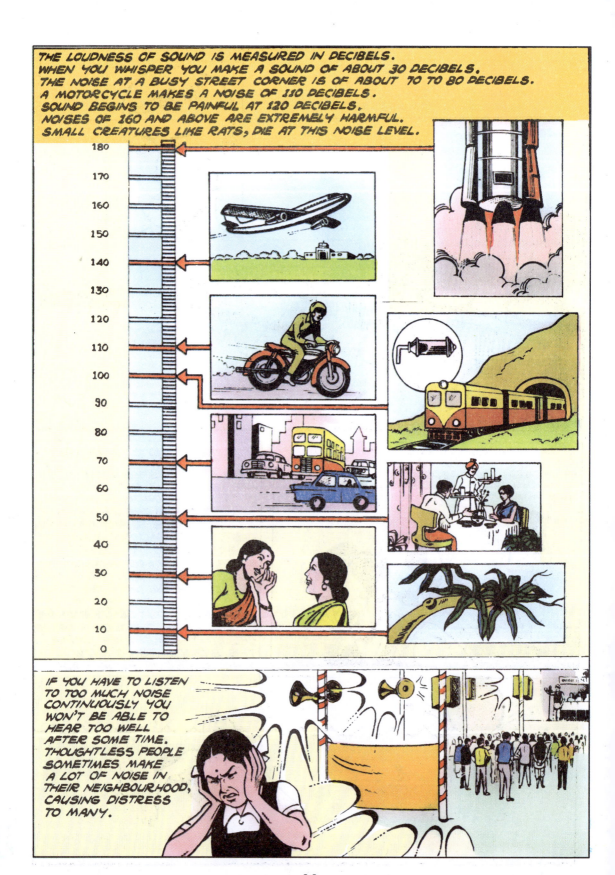

THE LOUDNESS OF SOUND IS MEASURED IN DECIBELS.
WHEN YOU WHISPER YOU MAKE A SOUND OF ABOUT 30 DECIBELS.
THE NOISE AT A BUSY STREET CORNER IS OF ABOUT 70 TO 80 DECIBELS.
A MOTORCYCLE MAKES A NOISE OF 110 DECIBELS.
SOUND BEGINS TO BE PAINFUL AT 120 DECIBELS.
NOISES OF 160 AND ABOVE ARE EXTREMELY HARMFUL.
SMALL CREATURES LIKE RATS, DIE AT THIS NOISE LEVEL.

180
170
160
150
140
130
120
110
100
90
80
70
60
50
40
30
20
10
0

IF YOU HAVE TO LISTEN TO TOO MUCH NOISE CONTINUOUSLY YOU WON'T BE ABLE TO HEAR TOO WELL AFTER SOME TIME. THOUGHTLESS PEOPLE SOMETIMES MAKE A LOT OF NOISE IN THEIR NEIGHBOURHOOD, CAUSING DISTRESS TO MANY.

ECHOES

Script : Luis M. Fernandes
Illustrations : Anand Mande

SOUND CAN BE REFLECTED. AN ECHO IS SOUND REPEATED BY REFLECTION.

ECHOES ARE USEFUL TO BOTH MAN AND BEAST. OIL EXPLORERS FOR EXAMPLE, MAKE USE OF ECHOES. AN UNDERGROUND EXPLOSION IS SENT DOWNWARD AND BY STUDYING THE SORT OF ECHOES RECEIVED, THEY CAN TELL IF THERE IS OIL BELOW.

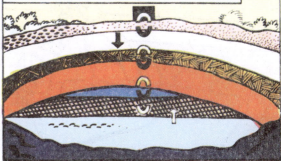

ECHOES ARE ALSO USED TO FIND THE DEPTH OF THE OCEAN. THE DEPTH IS FOUND BY MEASURING THE TIME BETWEEN SENDING OUT A SOUND SIGNAL AND RECEIVING THE ECHO REFLECTED FROM THE OCEAN BED.

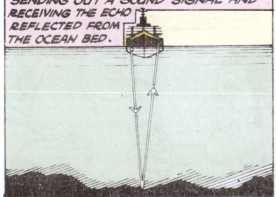

SOME BATS FIND THEIR FOOD AND THEIR WAY ABOUT BY USING ECHOES. BY MAKING HIGH-PITCHED SQUEAKS, THE SOUND WAVES WHICH BOUNCE BACK FROM OBJECTS TELL THEM WHAT IS IN THEIR PATH.

THESE MUSICIANS ARE PLAYING VERY WELL BUT THE MAN LISTENING TO THEM IS ALMOST DEAFENED BY THE ECHOES.

THE ECHOES CAN BE REDUCED BY PADDING THE WALLS, HANGING CURTAINS AND USING PADDED SEATS. THE CURTAINS AND THE SEATS WILL ABSORB SOME OF THE ECHOES. PEOPLE TOO ABSORB ECHOES. THERE ARE FEWER ECHOES IN A FULL HALL.

The Polite Miser

Illustrations : Ram Waeerkar

Readers' Choice

Based on a story sent by
Sanjay Kumar Jain,
Hyderabad

CHANDULAL WAS A MISER, BUT HE WAS ALWAYS POLITE TO HIS GUESTS.

WOULD YOU LIKE TO HAVE SOME TEA?

NO, THANK YOU.

GOOD.

WHAT ABOUT YOU? WOULD YOU LIKE TO HAVE SOME TEA?

YES, PLEASE!

BRING A TUMBLER OF TEA FOR UNCLE, LALLA.

AS LALLA TURNED TO GO IN—

HEY WAIT!

WOULD YOU LIKE GUR IN YOUR TEA OR SUGAR?

SUGAR OF COURSE. AND FOUR SPOONS OF IT!

AND WOULD YOU LIKE IT HOT OR COLD?

COLD? DID YOU SAY COLD TEA? WHY WOULD ANYONE WANT TO DRINK COLD TEA?

ONE MIGHT AS WELL DRINK WATER!

AH! SO YOU PREFER WATER.

LALLA, BRING A GLASS OF WATER. UNCLE HAS CHANGED HIS MIND...

!

Kalia
THE CROW

Script:
LUIS

Illustrations :
PRADEEP SATHE

AHHA, THERE'S A DEER COMING THIS WAY.

?

BABLOO!

WHERE'S THE HONEYCOMB YOU STOLE FROM MY CAVE, YOU RASCAL.

I...I... PUT ME DOWN. I'LL TELL YOU.

COME BACK, YOU THIEF!

CHAMATAKA IS IN TROUBLE AGAIN WITH BABLOO. BUT THAT JACKAL CAN TAKE CARE OF HIMSELF!

I SAW SOMETHING GO INTO THAT CAVE, BABLOO.

IT MAY HAVE BEEN CHAMATAKA... OR JUST A RABBIT.

I HATE TO LET THIS RABBIT GO. BUT IT'S THE ONLY WAY TO SAVE MY SKIN.

RUN HOME, KEECHU!

YOU CAN COME OUT TOO, CHAMATAKA.

EH!

DON'T BE AFRAID. BABLOO ISN'T HERE. I WAS JUST TALKING TO MYSELF.

WHAT!

FOOLED BY A CROW... BAH!

It's magic!

Wonder Bridge:
Challenge someone to make a piece of paper support a glass atop two spaced glasses.

Secret:
Fold the paper concertina-wise. It's strong enough to carry the glass!

Disappearing Pencil:
Place a pencil under a handkerchief. Toss the handkerchief aside and the pencil is gone!!

Secret:
As soon as you've placed the pencil under the handkerchief, extend your fore-finger to make it appear to be the pencil holding up the handkerchief.

At the same time, drop the pencil down your sleeve. When the handkerchief is removed, the pencil is gone! Remember, magic means practice and practice builds your confidence in the art of magic.

4 Coins to 5:
Set up four coins on a table in front of you. Count them off so that there can be no mistake about the fact that there are only four coins on the table.

Now slide these coins off the table and — voilà — you have five!

Secret:
Under the table there is a fifth coin which you have attached with a piece of soap. While you are gathering the four coins from the table top, simply reach under the table with your fingers, palming the fifth coin. A neat trick.

Amaze and astonish your friends with these astounding tricks. Easy to do but hard to believe.

And here's a trick that's most simple to do. Open a State Bank Savings Account in your name. If you are below 10, ask Daddy to open an Account for you. Put in your pocket money. And all the gift money you receive. And then watch your savings double and even treble as you grow.

Saving can be fun!

State Bank *
Security is a warm feeling

73

THE CLEVER GOAT

Illustrations:
M. Mohandas

Story sent by G.S. Ramakrishna, Hyderabad

A KID ONCE WANDERED AWAY FROM THE FLOCK.

OH, NO! A WOLF!

AAAHAA! I'M GOING TO EAT YOU UP.

A- ARE YOU SO HUNGRY?

CAN'T YOU WAIT TILL EVENING?

EVENING? WHY?

I'LL BE EATING GRASS THE WHOLE DAY SO I'LL BE VERY MUCH FATTER BY EVENING.

IS THAT SO?

ALL RIGHT, GO! I'LL WAIT HERE FOR YOU IN THE EVENING.

A LITTLE LATER—

OH, NO! A LION!

JUST THEN, SHE SAW SOME PUMPKINS GROWING IN A FIELD NEAR BY. SHE BROKE ONE OPEN.

THEN ENTERING IT . . .

. . . SHE MADE TWO HOLES IN THE TOP HALF . . .

. . . AND ROLLED AWAY . . .

GOODOO

. . . MAKING A GREAT DEAL OF NOISE.

GOODOO

GOODOO GOODOO

W-WHAT'S THAT?

GOODOO

A MONSTER! YIEEEE!

WHEN SHE REACHED THE TIGER—

GOODO

EE-YEOW!

THE LION TOO, WAS TERRIFIED BY THE SIGHT. HE RAN AWAY SO FAST...

...THAT HE TRIPPED AND BROKE A LEG.

FINALLY, ONLY THE WOLF WAS LEFT. AS THE PUMPKIN ROLLED TOWARDS HIM —

WH...WHO'S THAT? I'D BETTER GET OUT OF THE WAY AND TAKE A BETTER LOOK.

IT'S JUST A PUMPKIN! AND THERE'S SOMEONE IN IT!

COULD IT BE THE KID? I'LL SOON FIND OUT.

THE JUNGLE SCHOOL

SCRIPT: LUIS M. FERNANDES
ILLUSTRATIONS: PRADEEP SATHE

CHAMATAKA, I'VE GOT A LETTER FROM ONE OF MY ADMIRERS.

YOUR ADMIRERS!

ARE YOU SURE IT'S FOR YOU AND NOT FOR ME?

I AM SURE! IT'S FROM A SWEET LITTLE GIRL.

SHE WRITES... YOU TOO, LISTEN, KALIA.

I'M LISTENING.

SHE WRITES: "MY DEAR DOOB-DOOB..."

DID YOU HEAR THAT?

YES, YES. GO ON!

"MY DEAR DOOB-DOOB, HOW DID YOU EVER GET SUCH STRONG BEAUTIFUL TEETH..."

STRONG, BEAUTIFUL TEETH? HEE HEE HEE!

HEE HEE HEE HOO HOO HOO!

HE'S JEALOUS!

WELL, AREN'T YOU GOING TO TELL OUR READERS HOW YOU CAME TO HAVE SUCH STRONG BEAUTIFUL TEETH...?

AH, YES!

MY TEETH ARE SO STRONG AND BEAUTIFUL BECAUSE I KEEP THEM CLEAN...

ALL YOU HAVE TO DO TO KEEP YOUR TEETH CLEAN IS TO KEEP YOUR MOUTH OPEN...

WHEN I DO THAT, TINY BIRDS HOP IN AND EAT THE BITS OF FOOD STUCK TO MY TEETH.

DO THEY CLEAN YOUR TEETH? I THOUGHT THEY CLEANED ONLY YOUR TONGUE.

ANYWAY, I DON'T THINK HUMAN BEINGS CAN CLEAN THEIR TEETH THAT WAY.

WHY NOT?

FOR ONE THING, THE BIRDS WOULD NEVER GO NEAR THEM. SECONDLY, THEIR MOUTHS ARE NOT AS LARGE AS YOURS.

HUMAN BEINGS KEEP THEIR TEETH CLEAN BY BRUSHING THEM WITH TOOTHPASTE OR TOOTH POWDER...

···TWICE A DAY.

TWICE? WHY SO MANY TIMES?

WELL, THEY EAT A LOT OF SWEETS AND STARCH.

THE SWEETS ESPECIALLY ARE VERY DANGEROUS. IF ALLOWED TO REMAIN IN THE MOUTH THEY PRODUCE ACIDS WHICH ROT THE TEETH.

SO MY ADMIRERS··· I MEAN OUR READERS, SHOULD NOT EAT SWEETS.

OH, THEY CAN EAT SWEETS.

BUT THEY SHOULD RINSE THEIR MOUTHS AFTER EATING THEM. AND BRUSH THEIR TEETH BEFORE GOING TO BED.

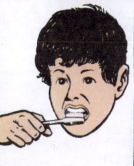

SO YOU SEE READERS, I HAVE SUCH STRONG BEAUTIFUL TEETH BECAUSE I KEEP THEM CLEAN.

···AND BECAUSE IF YOU LOSE A TOOTH, YOU GET ANOTHER ONE.

HUMAN BEINGS ARE NOT SO LUCKY. IF THEY LOSE A PERMANENT TOOTH THEY CAN'T GROW ANOTHER.

"MY DEAR DOOB DOOB, HOW DID YOU EVER GET SUCH STRONG BEAUTIFUL TEETH···" HEH-HEH.

ALL ABOUT TEETH

WHEN YOU SMILE, PEOPLE SEE THE CROWNS OF YOUR TEETH. NEITHER YOU NOR THEY CAN SEE THE ROOTS OF YOUR TEETH, AS THE ROOTS ARE HIDDEN BY THE GUMS.

BUT EVERY TOOTH IS MADE UP OF A CROWN AND ROOT, OR ROOTS.

THE ROOTS HOLD THE TEETH IN PLACE IN THE JAW.

EVERY TOOTH HAS A SOFT CENTRE CALLED PULP.

THE PULP IS MADE OF NERVES AND BLOOD VESSELS.

THE PULP IS WELL PROTECTED BY A HARD SUBSTANCE CALLED DENTINE.

BESIDES DENTINE, THE CROWN IS COVERED BY ENAMEL. ENAMEL IS THE HARDEST SUBSTANCE YOU CAN FIND IN YOUR BODY.

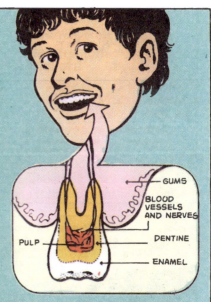

GUMS
BLOOD VESSELS AND NERVES
PULP
DENTINE
ENAMEL

PSSST...READERS, HERE'S HOW YOU CAN GET HOLES IN YOUR TEETH...AND ALSO TOOTHACHE.

IF YOU WANT HOLES IN YOUR TEETH, THE FIRST THING YOU HAVE TO DO IS GET RID OF THE ENAMEL ON THE CROWNS OF YOUR TEETH.

HOW DO YOU GET RID OF THE ENAMEL?

EASY.

ALL YOU DO IS LET PIECES OF FOOD, ESPECIALLY SWEETS, STAY BETWEEN YOUR TEETH AFTER YOU'VE EATEN.

YOU MAY THINK YOUR MOUTH IS CLEAN. BUT IT IS ALWAYS FULL OF BACTERIA. BACTERIA PRODUCE ACIDS OUT OF THE FOOD STUCK BETWEEN YOUR TEETH.

WHAT DO THE ACIDS DO?

THEY DISSOLVE A LITTLE OF THE ENAMEL.

IF YOU DO NOT CLEAN YOUR TEETH THE ENAMEL WILL BE GRADUALLY EATEN AWAY BY THE ACIDS FORMED IN THE MOUTH.

ONCE THE ENAMEL IS GONE, THE BACTERIA CAN GET AT THE LAYER UNDERNEATH IT, THE DENTINE.

IF NOT STOPPED THEY'LL EAT THEIR WAY THROUGH THE DENTINE RIGHT UP TO THE PULP.

NOW YOU HAVE A NICE HOLE IN YOUR TOOTH.

EVERY TIME YOU DRINK SOMETHING TOO COLD OR EAT SOMETHING TOO HOT, THE NERVES IN THE PULP WILL GET IRRITATED AND CAUSE A TOOTHACHE.

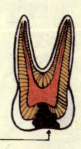

HOLE FORMED IN TOOTH

THE COBBLER

Idea by :
Appa Swami

Illustrations :
V.B. Halbe

NOW MY BUSINESS MAY PICK UP.

A. Siva
Rama
Kumar

My young friends,

One day a scorpion fell from a tree into a river and began shouting for help.

A turtle heard the scorpion's cries and swam to its aid.
The scorpion scrambled onto the turtle's back.
As the turtle was swimming toward the shore the scorpion bit the turtle's neck. "Don't do that," said the turtle.
But a little later, the scorpion bit it again.

"Why do you keep biting me?" asked the turtle, annoyed.
"I have a habit of biting," said the scorpion. "I cannot change my nature."
"And I have a habit of swimming underwater," said the turtle and dived under. The scorpion was drowned, and all because he could not control his bad habits.
This story has been sent by A. Siva Rama Kumar of Hyderabad.

Affectionately yours,

Uncle Pai

Mooshik
From an idea suggested by Sanjay M. Belurker, Panaji

(You don't have to draw the pictures when you send Mooshik ideas.)

Readers Write...

I am 55 years young. When the children's library in our garage for the area children was closed down due to unavoidable reasons and the books sold and the money given to charity, I continued to buy *Amar Chitra Katha* and *Tinkle*. These are for my grandchildren, they are too small to read them now, but there is always a fight for the first chance between the other three children — me, my 30-year-young doctor son and 22-year-young daughter-in-law. Tinkle has clean humorous stories and educative articles which appeal to both young and old.

Dr. (Mrs.) L. Pai
Hyderabad

You gave a good description of the Telescope in your issue No. 30, but you didn't write the meaning of the word. The world 'telescope' means 'seeing far away'.

Priyesh Bheda
Bombay

From a monthly
TINKLE became a fortnightly.

It may become a weekly
And some day a daily !

Amruth Valli
Aurangabad

See and smile
Based on an idea suggested by Amar A. Heblekar, Goa

EXPLORING THE SEAS

Script :
Padmini Rao Banerjee
Illustrations:
Makara

MEN HAVE BEEN DIVING FOR CENTURIES...

...TO COLLECT SPONGES AND OYSTERS.

A DIVER CAN HOLD HIS BREATH FOR A MINUTE AND A HALF, AT THE MOST. AFTER THAT, HE REQUIRES FRESH AIR.

SOME EARLY SWIMMERS USED HOLLOW REEDS AS BREATHING TUBES SO THAT THEY COULD STAY UNDERWATER LONGER.

LATER CAME THE IDEA OF USING AIR BAGS MADE OF ANIMAL HIDES. THE DIVER CARRIED A BAG WITH HIM UNDERWATER AND BREATHED THE AIR THROUGH A TUBE.

MEN USED OTHER METHODS TOO TO GO DOWN INTO THE WATER. ALEXANDER THE GREAT FOR EXAMPLE, ONCE HAD HIMSELF LOWERED INTO THE SEA IN A BARREL.

THE WORLD'S FIRST SUBMARINE WAS BUILT BY A DUTCHMAN, CORNELIUS VAN DREBBEL. IT WAS LAUNCHED IN 1624 ON THE RIVER THAMES IN ENGLAND. KING JAMES I IS SAID TO HAVE GONE FOR A SHORT RIDE IN IT.

IN 1715, AN ENGLISHMAN, JOHN LETHBRIDGE BUILT A DIVING BARREL SHAPED TO HOLD A MAN, WHICH COULD DESCEND TO 23 M.

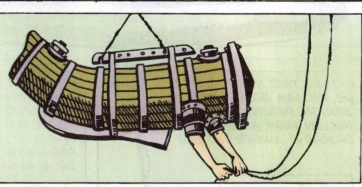

THE FIRST DIVING SUIT WAS CREATED BY A GERMAN IN 1819.

IT WAS IMPROVED THROUGH THE YEARS. THIS IS WHAT A MODERN DEEP-SEA DIVER WEARS. AIR IS PUMPED TO HIM THROUGH AN AIR PIPE, AND HE CAN TALK TO THE PEOPLE ON TOP THROUGH A TELEPHONE CABLE.

THE DEEP-SEA DIVER CAN DESCEND TO 100 METRES OR MORE.

THE AIR HOSE IS A NUISANCE WHEN THE DIVER IS MOVING AROUND. NOWADAYS, DIVERS WHO DO NOT WANT TO GO TOO DEEP CARRY AIR WITH THEM IN AIR CYLINDERS. THESE DIVERS WEAR TIGHT-FITTING RUBBER SUITS AND LARGE FLIPPERS ON THEIR FEET TO HELP THEM SWIM FASTER. KNOWN AS SKIN-DIVERS OR SCUBA DIVERS, THEY CANNOT GO AS DEEP OR REMAIN DOWN AS LONG AS THE DEEP-SEA DIVER.

AS DIVING DRESS IMPROVED, SO DID SUBMARINES. A MODERN NUCLEAR SUBMARINE CAN STAY UNDERWATER FOR MONTHS TOGETHER AND PROBABLY GO DOWN TO A DEPTH OF 700 M OR MORE.

IN 1934, TWO SCIENTISTS, DR. WILLIAM BEEBE AND OTIS BARTON, DESCENDED IN A HOLLOW IRON BALL TO A DEPTH OF 1000 M UNDER THE SEA.

IN 1960, A DIVING CRAFT CALLED A BATHYSCAPHE DESCENDED MORE THAN 10 KM INTO THE PACIFIC OCEAN. THE BATHYSCAPHE WAS INVENTED BY A SWISS PROFESSOR OF PHYSICS, DR. AUGUSTE PICCARD.

IN 1962, IN AN EXPERIMENT KNOWN AS THE CONSHELF II, SEVEN MEN LIVED FOR A MONTH SEVERAL METRES DEEP IN THE RED SEA. THEY LIVED IN THREE DIFFERENT HOUSES. THE HOUSES WERE SUPPLIED WITH POWER, LIGHT AND AIR FROM SHIPS ON THE SURFACE.

SINCE THE CONSHELF EXPERIMENT, SCIENTISTS HAVE STAYED IN THE SEA FOR AS LONG AS TWO MONTHS. PERHAPS A DAY MAY COME WHEN MAN WILL BE ABLE TO LIVE PERMANENTLY UNDER THE SEA!

THIS IS WHAT THE MAIN HOUSE LOOKED LIKE.

HIS SILENCE PAID

Illustrations
Ashok Dongre

Based on a story sent by
Saifuddin Topiwalla, Bombay

A MAN, DRIVING HIS HORSE-CART THROUGH A NARROW VILLAGE LANE, SUDDENLY LOST CONTROL...

...AND THE CART WENT HURTLING DOWN THE LANE.

MOVE TO THE SIDE! PLEASE MOVE TO THE SIDE!

MOVE TO THE SIDE, I SAY!

EEEE HI HI HI EE

HELP! HELP!

LOOK WHAT YOU'VE DONE! YOU'VE HURT MY BOY! I'LL TAKE YOU TO COURT FOR THIS!

89

LATER IN COURT—

MY LORD, THIS MAN PURPOSELY KNOCKED MY BOY DOWN WITH HIS CART!

IS THAT TRUE? DID YOU PURPOSELY KNOCK THE BOY DOWN?

THE JUDGE REPEATED THE QUESTION BUT THE MAN LOOKED BLANKLY AT THE JUDGE.

I AM ASKING YOU A QUESTION! WHY DON'T YOU ANSWER?

ON THE ROAD HE WAS SHOUTING: "MOVE TO THE SIDE! MOVE TO THE SIDE!" AND NOW HE'S NOT SAYING ANYTHING!

DID YOU HEAR THAT MY LORD? I KEPT ON SHOUT-ING TO EVERYONE TO GET OFF THE ROAD. I DID NOT HURT THE BOY ON PURPOSE.

YOU MAY GO— SHE HAS NO CASE AGAINST YOU!

THE WICKED CROW

Story by : Dnyanada Naik
Illustrations : M. Mohandas

ONE DAY A CROW CAUGHT HOLD OF A WREN.

I'M GOING TO EAT YOU UP!

SPARE ME PLEASE... PLEASE SPARE ME!

WHY SHOULD I?

I HAVE A LITTLE DAUGHTER. WHO WILL TAKE CARE OF HER?

AH...HA! SHE HAS A TENDER, LITTLE DAUGHTER. A BETTER MEAL THAN THIS TOUGH, OLD MOTHER.

WELL, I'LL BE KIND JUST THIS ONCE.

I WON'T EAT YOU.. I'LL EAT YOUR DAUGHTER! GET HER READY. I'LL BE BACK IN SEVEN DAYS.

A WEEK LATER —

MOTHER WREN! HERE I AM — BRING YOUR DAUGHTER TO ME...

YOUR BEAK IS FILTHY. IT WILL SPOIL THE TASTE OF YOUR MEAL. BRING SOME WATER AND I'LL CLEAN IT.

THE CROW FLEW OFF TO THE STREAM.

STREAM, STREAM! GIVE ME SOME WATER TO CARRY BACK TO MOTHER WREN.

I'LL GIVE YOU SOME WATER. BRING A POT.

THE CROW WENT AND ASKED THE POTTER FOR A POT.

MY POTS NEED TO BE BAKED. BRING ME SOME FIRE.

THE CROW RUSHED OFF IN SEARCH OF FIRE.

FIRE, FIRE! COME WITH ME TO THE POTTER.

MOST WILLINGLY. TAKE ME ALONG.

THE SILLY CROW RUSHED TO THE FIRE AND...

AAAH

MOTHER WREN LIVED ON HAPPILY WITH HER DAUGHTER.

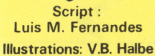

Shikari Shambu

Script :
Luis M. Fernandes
Illustrations: V.B. Halbe

* Refer to the footnote under the Editor's Note

MEET THE
PORTUGUESE MAN-OF-WAR

Script : Ashvin

Illustration: Pradeep Sathe

IN THE 18TH CENTURY SOME SAILORS SAW A STRANGE CREATURE IN THE SEA. IT WAS 30 CM. LONG AND 15 CM. WIDE. IT HAD A SAIL-LIKE CREST AND REMINDED THE SAILORS OF A PORTUGUESE BATTLESHIP OF THAT TIME. SO THEY NAMED THE CREATURE, PORTUGUESE MAN-OF-WAR.

HERE IS A SMACK (GROUP) OF THEM. THEY VARY IN COLOUR BUT ALL OF THEM HAVE A GAS-FILLED BLADDER WHICH FLOATS ABOVE WATER. ON THE TOP OF THE BLADDER IS A CREST...

SOMETIMES THE CREST GETS CAUGHT IN A WIND AND THEN THE PORTUGUESE MAN-OF-WAR IS DRIVEN HELPLESSLY THROUGH THE WATER.

BUT THE CREATURE CAN DEFLATE ITS BLADDER IF NECESSARY...

...AND RE-INFLATE IT WITHIN MINUTES.

WHAT YOU SEE HERE IS JUST A PART OF THE CREATURE.

NO. 39

Rs. 2.50

TINKLE

THE CHILDREN'S MONTHLY FROM THE HOUSE OF AMAR CHITRA KATHA

THE MAGIC POT

HOW CATS CAME INTO BEING

MEET THE CAT

SOUREN ROY

Based in Kolkata, Souren Roy was one of the first freelance artists to work with Amar Chitra Katha and *Tinkle*. His quirky art style set him apart from other artists. The domination of black in his art made his illustrations look stunning in black and white. This sure made the colourists grumble ever so often.

Souren Roy had a knack for drawing things the way they were. He didn't believe in beautifying his characters. His princesses were never unnaturally beautiful, neither were his warriors extremely handsome. His art reflected the world as he saw it.

Though he occasionally drew animals, he was marvellous with human characters. This was aided by the fact that he had a brilliant eye for details. The clothes his characters wore, their expressions and body language made his art very realistic and believable.

Since he was from Kolkata his knowledge of the region and the people there was extensive. He was the go-to artist for any stories based in Bengal. If *Tinkle* had any Bengali folk tales, Souren Roy would be the first choice for an artist.

HERE IS A FULL PICTURE OF A PORTUGUESE MAN-OF-WAR.

THE CREATURE HAS NO BONES. IT HAS NEITHER EYES, NOR EARS, NOR LIMBS.

IN FACT IT IS NOT ONE ANIMAL, BUT IS MADE UP OF A WHOLE COLONY OF TINY ANIMALS CALLED 'POLYPS' WHICH BEHAVE LIKE ONE INDIVIDUAL.

LET US SEE HOW THE CO-OPERATIVE COLONY WORKS.

LOOK! A FISH IS GOING TOWARDS THE PORTUGUESE MAN-OF-WAR.

AS YOU HAVE SEEN, SOME OF THEM ARE RESPONSIBLE FOR KEEPING THE COLONY AFLOAT.

THE SHORT TENTACLES EAT AND DIGEST FOOD WHILE THE LONG ONES (THEY CAN BE 10 M. LONG) CAPTURE PREY.

THE PREY IS STUNG AND HELD.

THE STINGING TENTACLES NOW CONTRACT...

...DRAWING THE PREY UP TO WHERE THE FEEDING POLYPS ARE WAITING FOR IT. THEY DON'T CHEW THE FOOD BUT POUR DIGESTIVE JUICES ON THE PREY AND DIGEST IT.

THE STING OF THE PORTUGUESE MAN-OF-WAR CAN BE DANGEROUS TO MAN. ITS POISON IS ALMOST AS POWERFUL AS A COBRA'S VENOM.

OFTEN SMALL FISH TRAVEL WITH THE PORTUGUESE MAN-OF-WAR, LIVING OFF ITS PREY.

THESE FISH ARE SILVERY WITH BRIGHT BLUE STRIPES.

FOR SOME STRANGE REASON THE PORTUGUESE MAN-OF-WAR DOESN'T HURT THIS PARTICULAR VARIETY OF FISH. AND THE FISH FEEL SAFE AMONG THE DEADLY TENTACLES.

DESPITE ITS STING THE PORTUGUESE MAN-OF-WAR IS EATEN BY SEVERAL ANIMALS. ONE OF THEM IS THE LOGGERHEAD TURTLE.

SOMETIMES IN STRONG WINDS THOUSANDS OF THE CREATURES ARE CAST UP ON SHORE. THE TENTACLES SOON DRY UP ON LAND.

EVEN WHEN DRY THE STINGING CELLS ARE DANGEROUS AND PRODUCE A RED WEAL ON THE SKIN LIKE A SEVERE BURN. SO BEWARE OF THEM.

WHEN A PORTUGUESE MAN-OF-WAR DIES IT SHEDS ITS EGGS AND SPERM INTO THE SEA. THE EGGS ARE THEN FERTILIZED AND FROM EACH OF THEM ONE LARVA IS FORMED.
THESE GROW FIRST INTO A GAS-FILLED BLADDER. AND THEN BIT BY BIT, THE ENTIRE COLONY OF POLYPS GROWS TO FORM A MATURE JELLYFISH.

The Naughty Smile

Story: Raj Kinger
Illustrations: Ram Waeerkar

LALIT WAS A VERY NAUGHTY BOY.

LALIT LAUGHED AND LAUGHED AND LAUGHED...

...TILL, SUDDENLY, HIS SMILE BROKE AWAY FROM HIS LIPS —

LALIT WAS VERY HAPPY TO GET HIS SMILE BACK.

THE PRIZE — WINNING ENTRY* FROM ANIRUDDHA JOSHI:

The tiger whose tail had been cut off was worried that the long-legged one would recognize him since he was the only one without a tail and that he would catch him again. So he decided to cut off the tail of another tiger. Thus one night he went and cut off the tail of the leader while he was sleeping. The leader screamed and got up, but it was too late. His tail was already lost. Now the leader was worried that the long-legged one would mistake him for the first tiger because he was also now without a tail.

So both these tigers decided to cut off the tails of two more tigers while they were asleep. These two then joined hands with the previous two, and thus the four tigers cut off the tails of four more; then eight more and so on.

And after a few days there was not a single tiger left in the jungle with a tail.

And none of these tail-less tigers dared to go and snatch a cow from the old lady's cowshed.

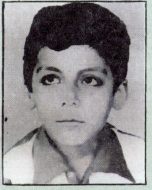

The first prize of Rs. 50 goes to **Aniruddha Joshi** 13, Jainiketan, 16th Road, Khar, Bombay 400 052

*

A consolation prize of Rs. 25 has been awarded to **Mamata Shende** Tata Housing Colony Type II/28, Chembur, Bombay 400 074

*Refer to the footnote under the Editor's Note

IF THEY SENSE ANY DANGER, SAY FROM A WILD CAT, THEY FLY AWAY.

THE TIMID, SILENT, DULL-COLOURED JACANA...

... LOOKS VERY DIFFERENT IN THE MONSOON, THE BREEDING SEASON.

THEN, BOTH MALES AND FEMALES BECOME BRIGHTER IN COLOUR AND GROW LONG TAIL-FEATHERS. THEY START CALLING OUT TO EACH OTHER: "TEWN, TEWN! TEWN!"

THESE FEMALES ARE FIGHTING OVER A HANDSOME MALE.

LOOK AT THE SPIKES ON THEIR WINGS. BOTH MALES AND FEMALES HAVE SPIKES AND THEY MAY USE THEM WHEN FIGHTING.

HE IS SMALLER THAN EITHER OF THEM. MALE JACANAS ARE ALWAYS SMALLER THAN THE FEMALES!

THE FEMALE WHO WINS GOES AWAY WITH THE MALE AND THEY MATE.

THEN THE PAIR BUILD A NEST. IT'S JUST A PILE OF WEEDS OR STEMS ON A LOTUS LEAF.

THE FEMALE LAYS FOUR EGGS ON THE FLOATING NEST. THE EGGS ARE GLOSSY AND LOOK AS IF THEY ARE VARNISHED. BECAUSE OF THIS GLOSS THE EGGS CANNOT GET WET.

THE MALE SITS ON THE EGGS TO INCUBATE THEM...

...WHILE THE FEMALE GOES IN SEARCH OF ANOTHER MALE.

AFTER MATING WITH ANOTHER, SHE LAYS FOUR EGGS FOR HIM TOO.

THE FEMALE STANDS GUARD ONLY WHEN HER MATES GO OUT TO FEED. SHE NEVER WARMS THE EGGS HERSELF. THE MALES HAVE TO DO THAT JOB THEMSELVES.

THE CHICKS HATCH AFTER TWO WEEKS. THEY ARE SO WELL-DEVELOPED THAT THEY CAN RUN IMMEDIATELY.

THE YOUNG ONES FIND THEIR FOOD THEMSELVES UNDER THE WATCHFUL EYE OF THE ADULTS...AND THEY GROW RAPIDLY. MEANWHILE, THE ADULT BIRDS LOSE THEIR TAIL-FEATHERS AND THE BRIGHT COLOURS FADE AWAY.

THE JACANA YOU'VE JUST READ ABOUT IS CALLED THE PHEASANT-TAILED JACANA.

THERE ARE OTHER SPECIES OF JACANA IN OTHER PARTS OF THE WORLD. BUT THEY ARE NOT AS COLOURFUL AS THE INDIAN ONES.

THE BRONZE-WINGED JACANA:

THIS IS ANOTHER SPECIES OF JACANA FOUND IN INDIA. THEIR HABITS ARE THE SAME AS THOSE OF THE PHEASANT-TAILED JACANA, BUT THEIR COLOURS DON'T CHANGE DURING THE BREEDING SEASON.

To Our Readers *

TINKLE SUBSCRIPTIONS :

All new subscriptions and renewals of the old ones are accepted at:

PARTHA BOOKS DIVISION
Nav Prabhat Chambers, Ranade Road, Dadar, Bombay 400 028.

The annual subscription rate for 24 issues is Rs. 72/- per year (add Rs. 3/- on outstation cheques). Drafts/cheques/M.O. should be in favour of PARTHA BOOKS DIVISION.

All complaints pertaining to the old subscriptions (upto subscription No. 5000) should be addressed to India Book House Magazine Co., 249, D.N. Road, Bombay 400 001.

Readers' Contributions should be addressed to Editor, TINKLE, Mahalaxmi Chambers, (Basement), 22, Bhulabhai Desai Road, Bombay 400 026.

* Send a self-addressed stamped envelope if you want the story to be returned.
* Please do not send photographs until asked for.
* For "Readers' Choice" please send only folktales you have heard and not those you have read in books, magazines or textbooks. Rs. 25/- will be paid for every accepted contribution.

Mooshik :
Rs. 10/- will be paid for every original idea accepted.

This happened to me :
You can write on your own strange, thrilling, or amusing experience or adventure. Rs. 15/- will be paid for every accepted contribution.

Readers' Mail :
1. Mail your letters to: Tinkle, Post Bag No. 16541, Bombay 400 026.
2. Please give your address in your letters, if you want a reply.

TINKLE TRICKS AND TREATS :

1. Mail your entry to:
   Tinkle Competition Section,
   Post Bag No. 16541,
   Bombay 400 026.
2. The first 400 all-correct entries received by us will each win a copy of the AMAR INDIA WALL PAPER No. 16 dated August 1983.

Mooshik

From an idea suggested by Veena R. Lahoti.

* Refer to the footnote under the Editor's Note

- - - - CUT HERE - - - -

TTT-32

ENTRY FORM*

NAME _____

ADDRESS _____

STATE _____

PIN ☐ ☐ ☐ ☐ ☐ ☐

MY SOLUTIONS:

A _____

B _____

C _____

EDITOR'S CHOICE

My young friends,

The king of Devpur sought his guru's advice on every important matter.

Once it so happened that there were two candidates for the same job in the palace. The king sent both the men to his guru. The guru talked to them for a while. Then he gave one of them a sieve and the other a winnowing scoop and sent them back to the king.

"What could the guru have meant by this?" the king asked his minister. "I'll have to give it some thought, Maharaj. I'll need some time," replied the minister.

When the minister returned home, he saw his wife winnowing husks away from the grain in a winnowing scoop. Later he saw her sifting flour in a sieve. In a flash, he understood.

He went back to the king. "My lord, the man who brought the winnowing scoop will retain the useful things and reject the useless. The one who brought the sieve will retain the useless things and reject the useful."

The king employed the candidate who came with the winnowing scoop.

Affectionately yours,

Uncle Pai

This story was sent in by Kumari Lilavati Kulkarni of Gulbarga

THE GREAT RACE

Illustrations: M. Mohandas

Based on a story sent by Santosh Kumar, Bombay

ONE DAY SOME VEGETABLES DECIDED TO HAVE A RACE. OLD MR. CABBAGE WAS SELECTED AS REFEREE.

ALL THOSE ENTERING THE RACE PLEASE STAND IN LINE.

WITH MY GLOWING HEALTH, I'M SURE TO BE THE FASTEST.

YOU! YOU WATCH ME!

I CAN RUN THE LONGEST.

HEH-HEH! YOU'RE BOTH TOO FAT.

I'LL OUTRUN BOTH OF YOU!

ON YOUR MARK...

...GET SET...

SUDDENLY—

BOOMCRASH

AAGH! I'VE HURT MYSELF.

HEH-HEH! NOW IS MY CHANCE TO WIN.

EVERYBODY WILL KNOW THAT I AM THE FASTEST VEGETABLE.

JUST THEN A PARROT HAPPENED TO BE FLYING BY AND SPOTTED THE CHILLI.

AHA, WHAT A DELICIOUS MEAL THAT FRESH GREEN CHILLI WILL MAKE.

OH NO! IT'S THE GREAT PARROT!

EEEEEE!

ONE BY ONE, ALL THE VEGETABLES WERE OUT OF THE RACE.

AND THE ONLY ONE WHO FINISHED THE RACE WAS THE HUMBLE ONION.

LONG LIVE THE ONION! HIP-HIP-HOORAY!

TINKLE TRICKS & TREATS* TTT—32

* Refer to the footnote under the Editor's Note

A **Strike a difference!**
Why is one of these instruments different from the others?

B **What is missing here?**

C **Whose feet are these?** Elephant • Camel • Platypus • Ostrich • Kangaroo
Match the name of the animal with its foot.

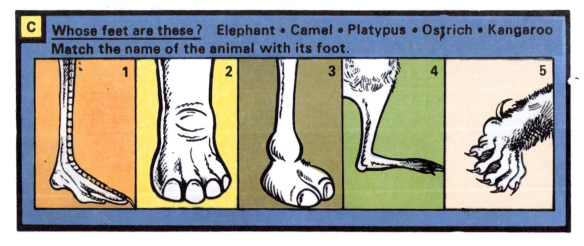

SOLUTIONS OF TTT-32

A. The flute. The others are string instruments while the flute is a wind instrument.

B. The nib of his pen is missing.

C. 1. Ostrich 2. Elephant 3. Camel 4. Kangaroo 5. Platypus

Fun with shadows

Ideas by Rajakaka

You will need : A table-lamp; a bare wall for a screen and your hands, of course !

You can have a poultry show in your house!
Stand a few feet away from a wall and arrange your hands and fingers in front of a lamp as shown to make the shadow of a hen.

A rooster needs a comb. You'll have to cut it out from a piece of stiff paper and hold it up as shown.

You need a cut-out for the chicken too. Make sure you cut out a hole where its eye should be.

Readers Write...

Sunrise, Sunset

The sun rises in the east
And sets in the west.
When the sun rises or sets
The colours of the sky
Are at their best.

There's red, there's orange,
There's also pink,
Spread around the sun
Like a ruby ring.

When the sun rises
I'm on my way to school,
I watch the sun
Throwing gold into the pool.

When the sun sets
I watch it go,
Till there are no traces left
Outside my window.

The sun has drowned,
But only for now—
Tomorrow I will watch it rise
With such colours — WOW!

Sonali Bhatia
Bombay

There was an all High School Quiz held in Madras recenty. In the last round our opponents were leading. They were asked to draw a comic picture; I drew one of Mooshik. They all began to laugh and our team got the prize!

Abdul Kareem
Madras

Once we children of Class II went on a picnic. I took 5 copies of TINKLE along to read. I sat with my teacher reading them under a tree. My teacher asked for one copy. I gave it to her and she liked it. She borrowed two and gave them back to me the next day. She really enjoyed TINKLE! I didn't know that even teachers like reading comics!

Priyanka Jhunjhunwala
New Delhi

Once we had gone to Tungeshwar which is near Bombay. It has a dense forest with a river flowing between the mountains. There is a small temple of Shiva. We were sitting in front of the temple. Cows were also sitting quietly. Suddenly the cows started running and they were very scared. Two bright eyes were coming towards us. We were stunned to see a leopard. We ran into the temple immediately and shut the doors.

Neeraj Tikku
Bombay

The Emperor's Reward

Script: Meera Ugra
Illustrations: Dilip Kadam

HUMAYUN, THE MUGHAL EMPEROR, WAS ONCE DEFEATED IN A BATTLE. HIS SOLDIERS FLED IN PANIC...

...AND HE, TOO, WAS SURROUNDED ON ALL SIDES.

WELL'...THAT'S THE ONLY WAY LEFT!

JAHANPANAH!

WHEN THEY REACHED THE OTHER SHORE—

WHO ARE YOU?

MY NAME IS NIZAM. I AM A WATER-CARRIER IN HUZOOR'S ARMY.

YOU HAVE SAVED MY LIFE.

HUMAYUN MADE HIS WAY TO AGRA.

AND THE NEXT DAY HE SUMMONED THE WATER-CARRIER TO THE PALACE.

COME FORWARD, NIZAM.

I AM A DEFEATED MAN. I HAVE NOTHING TO GIVE YOU...

...BUT MY THRONE.

Y-YOUR THRONE?!

WHAT DO I KNOW OF STATE MATTERS? MY LORD, PLEASE ...PLEASE...LET ME GO.

SIT DOWN, NIZAM!

AND, NIZAM, THE WATER-CARRIER, RULED ON THE THRONE OF AGRA FOR A DAY.

ONCE A RABBIT WAS DOZING UNDER A TREE.

ZZ

SUDDENLY HE WOKE UP —

A TIGER!

DESPERATELY, HE LOOKED AROUND FOR HELP. THEN—

AH!

WHAT ARE YOU DOING HERE?

I AM KEEPING WATCH OVER MY GRANDFATHER'S PRECIOUS GONG.

IT IS SAID THAT HE WHO CAN SOUND IT WILL GAIN GREAT POWERS. BUT NONE OF US SMALL RABBITS CAN REACH IT!

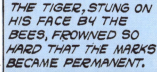

Kaviraj and his Neighbours

Illustrations: Ram Waeerkar

Readers' Choice

Story sent by
Anil Kumar Jaiswal,
Varanasi

KAVIRAJ, A POET, WANTED TO WRITE GREAT POEMS, BUT HE HAD NOISY NEIGHBOURS.

OH, THIS NOISE! I'LL GO INSIDE AND WRITE THERE.

BANG BANG BANG THACK

BUT WHEN HE WENT TO THE OTHER SIDE OF THE HOUSE—

SAA REE GAA MA

SOMETHING MUST BE DONE! OR THE WORLD WILL NOT KNOW WHAT A GREAT POET I AM!

HERE'S SOME MONEY. FIND ANOTHER PLACE TO LIVE IN.

DON'T WORRY. I'LL MOVE OUT OF HERE TOMORROW!

* Refer to the footnote under the Editor's Note

THE MOON —Our Strange Neighbour —1

Script : J.D. Isloor ● **Illustrations : Anand Mande**

WHEN GALILEO TURNED HIS TELESCOPE ON THE MOON FOR THE FIRST TIME IN 1609...

... HE WAS AMAZED TO SEE MOUNTAINS AND CRATERS AND PLAINS ON IT.

SOME OF THE MOUNTAIN PEAKS ARE OF GREAT HEIGHT. THE LUNAR MOUNTAIN, LEIBNITZ IS HIGHER THAN MT. EVEREST. THE CRATERS ARE OF VARIOUS SIZES — SOME AS SMALL AS PEANUTS, OTHERS SEVERAL KILOMETRES IN DIAMETER. THERE IS ONE FACTOR COMMON TO ALL THESE CRATERS : THEY ARE ALL CIRCULAR.

THE MOON IS OUR NEAREST NEIGHBOUR AND THE ONLY ONE EVER TO HAVE BEEN VISITED BY MAN.

IT IS ONLY ABOUT 3,84,360 KM. AWAY FROM US. IF IT WERE POSSIBLE TO LAY TRACKS BETWEEN THE EARTH AND THE MOON, IT WOULD TAKE A TRAIN, TRAVELLING AT AN AVERAGE SPEED OF 120 KM. PER HOUR, 130 DAYS TO REACH THE MOON.

YOU MAY CONSIDER THIS A VERY LONG DISTANCE, BUT COMPARED TO THE DISTANCES OF OTHER HEAVENLY BODIES THIS DISTANCE IS NOT MUCH.

SUN

MERCURY

MOON

EARTH

VENUS

THE MOON IS ROUGHLY A QUARTER OF THE SIZE OF THE EARTH. BUT AS FAR AS ITS WEIGHT IS CONCERNED, IT WOULD TAKE 81 MOONS TO EQUAL THE WEIGHT OF THE EARTH.

ALL OBJECTS THAT ARE DROPPED FROM A HIGH POINT OR THROWN UP WILL COME BACK TO EARTH ULTIMATELY. THE EARTH 'PULLS' THEM ALL. THIS PULL OF THE EARTH IS CALLED GRAVITY.

THE WEIGHT OF EVERYTHING DEPENDS ON GRAVITY. THIS MAN CANNOT LIFT THIS BAR-BELL WEIGHING 180 KGS.

BUT HE WOULD BE ABLE TO LIFT IT EASILY ON THE MOON BECAUSE THERE IT WOULD WEIGH ONLY 30 KGS. THE MOON'S GRAVITY OR PULLING POWER IS ONLY 1/6 TH THAT OF THE EARTH.

YOU CAN'T JUMP TOO HIGH ON THE EARTH, BECAUSE THE EARTH PULLS YOU DOWN VERY STRONGLY. IF YOU CAN JUMP 4 FEET HIGH HERE...

... ON THE MOON, YOU WOULD BE ABLE TO JUMP 24 FEET (6 X 4) BECAUSE EVEN THOUGH YOU WOULD BE SIX TIMES LIGHTER THERE, YOUR ENERGY WOULD REMAIN THE SAME.

IT IS DIFFICULT TO FALL ON THE MOON. THE ASTRONAUTS FOUND THAT IF THEY LOST THEIR BALANCE THEY BEGAN TO FALL IN SLOW MOTION, GIVING THEM PLENTY OF TIME TO REGAIN THEIR BALANCE.

Kalia
THE CROW

Script:
LUIS

Illustrations:
PRADEEP SATHE

ARE YOU CHAMATAKA?

YES.

DOOB-DOOB WANTS YOU TO COME OVER TO HIS HOUSE. HE'LL BE WAITING FOR YOU AT THE RIVER.

LET HIM WAIT...

...DOES HE THINK I'LL COME RUNNING WHENEVER HE CALLS ME?

I'VE BETTER THINGS TO DO.

?!

IT'S BABLOO!

ABOUT
SHIKARI SHAMBU

Cowardly Shikari Shambu and his sola topi (and his gloriously expressive moustache) have been a mainstay in *Tinkle* since 1983. How he came to join the pages of *Tinkle* is a tale in itself.

One of *Tinkle*'s competitors in 1983 was a magazine called *Target*. While this was largely a narrative magazine, it did carry a few comic pages. The most popular character from these comics was Moochwala, drawn by veteran cartoonist Ajit Ninan. Moochwala, as his name suggests, bore a large moustache and a piercing gaze, but was a bumbling detective.

Subba Rao, the co-founder of *Tinkle*, one day told the *Tinkle* editorial team very enthusiastically that he had found the answer to Moochwala. The inspiration had struck him while watching *I Love Lucy*, a popular comedy television show at the time. One of the characters in the show was a boastful but cowardly big-game hunter who found himself in hilarious misadventures. That is how Mr. Rao came up with the idea of Shambu for *Tinkle*.

Writer-editor Luis Fernandes wrote the first story for this character three days later. He named him Shambu, while Mr. Rao prefixed it with Shikari. However, Anant Pai, the founder editor of *Tinkle*, and writer-editor Kamala Chandrakant weren't comfortable with the title 'Shikari' or hunter. Wildlife conservation efforts were gathering steam, and there was a growing general consensus on the need to protect animals. But the name Shikari Shambu stuck, because it just seemed too good to let go. The editorial team therefore decided that Shambu would never shoot an animal, even though he carried a gun and the moniker of a hunter.

While Shambu and his antics seemed funny on paper, he turned out to be funnier when given a face and a form. In fact, Mr. Fernandes credits Shambu's popularity to the illustrations of Shambu's artist, Vasant Halbe. However, Mr. Halbe was not the team's first choice. Pradeep Sathe, the then Art Director, had suggested Mr. Halbe, but the Editorial team believed his cartoonish art style would be unsuitable. Mr. Sathe insisted and had Mr. Halbe produce several sketches for the character. One of the sketches was that of a man who wore a sola topi so low that it covered his eyes. Needless to say, the Editorial team immediately knew it had found Shambu's look.

Thus was born Shikari Shambu. In the quest to chase tigers, lions and bears, Shambu ended up being chased himself, always with comical and unexpected results. And after a few issues, the *Tinkle* team even decided to do away with his gun and Shambu truly became the embodiment of the most cowardly person to grace the pages of *Tinkle*.

THE MAGIC POT

Script : Meera Ugra
Illustrations : Ram Waeerkar

A MAN AND HIS WIFE WERE DIGGING IN THEIR VEGETABLE PATCH ONE DAY, WHEN SUDDENLY—

THANN THANN

THERE'S SOMETHING HERE!

IT'S A POT!

LET'S TAKE IT OUT.

IT'S SO HUGE.

...AND SO HEAVY, TOO.

130

OH! THIS IS TERRIBLE...

...SHE CAN'T STAY HERE! SHE WON'T!

BUT... WHERE WILL SHE GO?

WHY DID YOU HAVE TO PULL HER OUT! YOU SHOULD HAVE LEFT HER THERE.

AND NOT USE THE POT EVER AGAIN!

THROW HER IN!

SO THAT A THIRD WOMAN COMES OUT, EH?

STOP ARGUING. I AM FAMISHED!

HOW CAN YOU THINK OF EATING AT A TIME LIKE THIS!

BIRD-STRIKE

Based on material provided by
T.N. Prakash

Illustrations: Pradeep Sathe

IF YOU THROW A SMALL PEBBLE AT THE WINDSCREEN OF A PARKED CAR, THE GLASS IS NOT LIKELY TO BREAK.

BUT IF THE SAME PEBBLE WERE TO HIT THE CAR WHEN IT IS MOVING AT 80 K.P.H. THE PEBBLE MAY CRACK THE WINDSCREEN.

SPEED MAKES ALL THE DIFFERENCE.

IF A 5 KG. GOOSE WERE TO HIT AN AIRCRAFT TRAVELLING AT 800 K.P.H...

...THE BIRD COULD CRASH RIGHT THROUGH THE WINDSHIELD.

ANY CONTACT BETWEEN A MOVING AIRCRAFT AND A BIRD IS CALLED A BIRD-STRIKE.

SOMETIMES A PLANE RUNS INTO A FLOCK OF BIRDS...

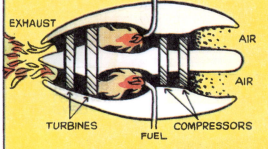

EXHAUST

AIR

AIR

TURBINES   FUEL   COMPRESSORS

...AND A BIRD GETS INTO THE ENGINE, BREAKING THE PARTS INSIDE.

OTHER MAJOR PARTS OF THE AIRCRAFT WHICH CAN BE DAMAGED BY BIRDS ARE THE TAIL, FIN, WINGS, NOSE, RADAR AND LANDING GEAR.

DIFFERENT BIRDS BEHAVE DIFFERENTLY WHEN AN AIRCRAFT APPROACHES.

CANADIAN GEESE, MALLARDS AND GULLS TRY TO OUTFLY THE AIRCRAFT...

...EAGLES SOMETIMES ATTACK...

...AND VULTURES FLY CLOSE BEHIND THE TAIL.

WHY CAN'T A PILOT TURN THE PLANE ASIDE WHEN HE SEES A BIRD FLYING TOWARDS IT?
THE ANSWER IS HE DOESN'T HAVE ENOUGH TIME TO DO SO.

HERE'S A BIRD APPROACHING A PLANE. THE BIRD IS 1000 METRES AWAY.
THE PILOT TAKES

0·1	SECONDS TO SEE THE BIRD
0·5	SECONDS TO RECOGNISE THE DANGER
1·0	SECOND TO DECIDE TO CHANGE DIRECTION
0·4	SECONDS TO REACH FOR THE CONTROLS
2·0	SECONDS FOR THE PLANE TO MOVE AWAY

TOTAL OF 4·0 SECONDS

BY THAT TIME THE PLANE AND THE BIRD HAVE ALREADY COLLIDED, BECAUSE IT TAKES THE PLANE ONLY 3·6 SECONDS TO COVER 1000 METRES.

SO, IT IS DIFFICULT FOR A PILOT TO AVOID HITTING A BIRD IN THE AIR, BUT HE MAY TAKE THE PRECAUTION OF STUDYING BIRD MAPS BEFORE TAKING OFF. BIRD MAPS SHOW THE ROUTES VARIOUS BIRDS TAKE WHILE MIGRATING.

MANY BIRD-STRIKES HOWEVER, OCCUR WHEN AN AIRCRAFT IS JUST TAKING OFF OR LANDING. SO IT IS NECESSARY TO KEEP BIRDS AWAY FROM AIRPORTS.

SOURCES OF DANGER

GARBAGE: GARBAGE DUMPS NEAR AIRPORTS ATTRACT BIRDS TO THE AREA.

THE WHITE BACKED VULTURE: THE BIRD RESPONSIBLE FOR MOST AIR ACCIDENTS IN INDIA.

How cats come into being

Script: Nira Benegal
Illustrations: Pradeep Sathe

EVERYONE ON BOARD NOAH'S ARK WAS SAFE —

BUT IT WAS BECOMING TOO CROWDED.

SOME OF THE CREATURES NOAH HAD ON BOARD, ESPECIALLY THE MICE, WERE MULTIPLYING TOO FAST.

SOON, THERE WON'T BE ENOUGH ROOM TO MOVE... BESIDES THEY EAT SO MUCH!

THE MERCHANT AND THE THIEF

Readers' Choice

Based on a story sent by Subhash Godakh, Ahmednagar

Illustrations : V. B. Halbe

THE MERCHANT, GHUNA, WAS ON A JOURNEY TO SONAI. ON THE WAY—

DO YOU MIND IF I ACCOMPANY YOU?

NOT AT ALL!

IN FACT, I WAS LOOKING FOR COMPANY.

THIS AREA IS INFESTED WITH THIEVES.

YOU ARE ABSOLUTELY RIGHT!

THAT NIGHT THEY STOPPED AT AN INN.

I AM VERY TIRED AND I'M GOING TO SLEEP.

NOW IS THE TIME TO RIFLE THROUGH HIS LUGGAGE...

BUT THE THIEF WAS DISAPPOINTED.

NOTHING!

THE NEXT MORNING —

ARE YOU CARRYING ANY MONEY WITH YOU?

THE WATCHFUL EYE

Illustrations: Ram Waeerkar

Readers' Choice

Based on a story sent by Iffat Rashid, Srinagar

VITHALRAO, THE RICH MERCHANT HAD A GLASS EYE.

IT'S A HOT NIGHT! I AM GOING TO SLEEP.

FAN ME!

HE TOOK OUT HIS GLASS EYE AND KEPT IT CAREFULLY ON A SIDE TABLE...

...AND WENT TO SLEEP.

THE NEXT DAY—

YOU LOOK SO TIRED EVERY MORNING. DON'T YOU SLEEP AT NIGHT?

HOW CAN I? I HAVE TO FAN THE MASTER THE WHOLE NIGHT.

YOU FOOL, YOU SHOULD GO TO SLEEP THE THE MOMENT HE CLOSES HIS EYES.

THAT'S THE TROUBLE. THE CUNNING MAN DOESN'T CLOSE BOTH EYES WHEN HE SLEEPS.

HE TAKES ONE OUT AND KEEPS IT ASIDE SO THAT IT CAN WATCH OVER ME!

My young friends,

Once there was a great flood which covered the whole earth. The story of this flood is to be found in the legends and mythologies of several peoples. An account of it is found in the Vedas and the Matsya Purana.

The story of the flood is found in the Bible too. God told Noah to build a large ship and to take on board his family and two members of every living thing on earth. Noah did as he was commanded.

Then it rained for forty days and forty nights and everything on earth perished in the water. Only Noah and those in the ship with him were saved.

Elsewhere in this issue there is a fanciful tale based on the story of Noah and the flood. Let me know how you like it.

Yours affectionately,

Uncle Pai

FROG

YOU'RE READING ABOUT KANGAROOS!

KANGAROO

WHAT DOES RAMAN SAY TO HIS TEACHER?

* Refer to the footnote under the Editor's Note

1. Mail your entry to:
   TINKLE
   Competition Section,
   P. Bag No. 16541
   Bombay 400 026

2.
   ● First prize — Rs. 50/-
   ● Second prize — Rs. 25/-
   ● Third prize — Rs. 15/-
   ● 10 Consolation prizes,
     Rs. 10/- each

3. Decision of the judges is final and binding. Names of the prize winners will be announced in TINKLE No. 43

Last date for receiving entries: August 20, 1983

- CUT HERE

ENTRY FORM*   Say it Yourself – 1

NAME _____   Answer: _____

_____   _____

ADDRESS _____   _____

_____   _____

_____   _____

STATE _____

PIN [ ][ ][ ][ ][ ][ ]

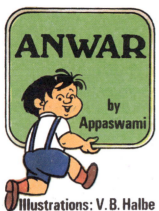

ANWAR

by
Appaswami

Illustrations: V. B. Halbe

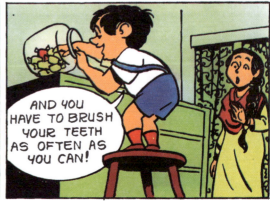

146

MEET THE CAT

Script : Ashvin

Illustrations : Pradeep Sathe

CATS ARE BEAUTIFUL AND GRACEFUL ANIMALS. KEEPING ONE AS A PET CAN BE A REWARDING EXPERIENCE.

THE KITTEN YOU BRING HOME SHOULD BE ABOUT 2 MONTHS OLD. IT'LL BE NERVOUS AND UNFRIENDLY FOR A FEW DAYS...

...BUT IF YOU TREAT IT WELL AND GIVE IT REAL AFFECTION, IT WILL SOON MAKE ITSELF COMFORTABLE.

AS EVERYONE KNOWS, CATS ARE VERY FOND OF MILK. GIVE YOUR CAT A SAUCER OF MILK TWICE A DAY.

COLLARS AND LEASHES ARE JUST NOT FOR THE CAT.

THEY NEED MEAT TOO AND THEY LOVE FISH.
BUT IT IS ADVISABLE TO COOK THE FISH BEFORE YOU GIVE IT TO YOUR KITTEN.

IF YOU'RE A STRICT VEGETARIAN, DON'T WORRY. YOUR CAT WILL LEARN TO CATCH MICE.

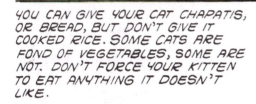

YOU CAN GIVE YOUR CAT CHAPATIS, OR BREAD, BUT DON'T GIVE IT COOKED RICE. SOME CATS ARE FOND OF VEGETABLES, SOME ARE NOT. DON'T FORCE YOUR KITTEN TO EAT ANYTHING IT DOESN'T LIKE.

IF YOU LIVE IN A MULTI-STOREYED BUILDING AND YOUR CAT CAN'T GO OUT FOR ITS TOILET THEN ARRANGE A LITTER BOX FILLED WITH SAND OR CHAFF. AFTER EVERY MEAL PICK YOUR KITTEN UP AND SET IT IN THE BOX. IT WILL SOON BE TOILET-TRAINED.

BUT PROVIDE IT WITH A BOWL OF CLEAN DRINKING WATER. AT ALL TIMES.

147

CATS DON'T HAVE TO BE BATHED. THEY LICK THEIR BODIES CLEAN WITH THEIR ROUGH TONGUES.

TO CLEAN THEIR EYES AND SNOUT THEY USE THEIR PAWS.

BUT THEY NEED HELP TO REMOVE PAINT OR GREASE FROM THEIR FUR.

COMB AND BRUSH YOUR CAT'S FUR EVERYDAY. YOUR CAT WILL LOVE IT. USE A WIDE-TOOTHED COMB FOR THE PURPOSE.

IF YOUR CAT DOESN'T GO OUT, KEEP A CARPET-COVERED POST WHICH IT CAN CLAW.

WHILE BRUSHING IF YOU FIND TICKS OR FLEAS IN ITS FUR, REMOVE THEM CAREFULLY WITH A TWEEZER.

CATS KEEP THEIR CLAWS SHARP BY SCRATCHING.

TAKE A BOX OR A BASKET, LINE IT WITH A PIECE OF BLANKET OR RUG AND KEEP IT IN A CORNER. IT'S YOUR CAT'S BED.

CATS SELECT VERY ODD AND FUNNY PLACES TO REST ON. IT CAN BE A WINDOW LEDGE, OR THE TOP OF A SHELF, SOME PARTICULAR CHAIR OR EVEN YOUR BED, IF YOU ALLOW IT.

TRY CHANGING THE POSITION OF THE BASKET IF YOUR CAT REFUSES TO SLEEP IN IT.

NEVER TEASE YOUR CAT BY PULLING AT ITS EARS OR TAIL OR WHISKERS.

...: AND IT HAS 30 SHARP TEETH IN ITS MOUTH— 16 IN THE UPPER JAW AND 14 IN THE LOWER JAW.

DON'T FORGET THAT YOUR CAT'S CUTE-LOOKING PAWS ARE WELL-EQUIPPED WITH RAZOR-SHARP CLAWS...

THE CAT IS CAPABLE OF USING BOTH THESE WEAPONS VERY EFFECTIVELY. REMEMBER, A CAT IS NOT AS TOLERANT AS A DOG.

ANOTHER THING ABOUT CATS —: HOWEVER WELL YOU MAY TREAT THEM, THEY'LL NEVER OBEY YOU OR TREAT YOU AS MASTER OR MISTRESS.

SOMEDAY, HOWEVER, YOUR CAT MAY BRING YOU A GIFT, A DEAD MOUSE OR SOMETHING OF THAT SORT. DON'T SCOLD IT. IT'S JUST TRYING TO THANK YOU FOR BEING SO GOOD TO IT.

IN COURSE OF TIME, YOU'LL BEGIN TO UNDERSTAND ALL THE VARIOUS MOODS OF YOUR CAT...

DEMANDING FOOD

CURIOSITY

ANGRY AND READY TO ATTACK

...AND YOU'LL GROW TO LOVE IT DESPITE ITS LACK OF DEVOTION TO YOU.

AT NIGHT YOUR CAT WILL WANT TO GO OUT. JUST FOR A STROLL OR TO HUNT MICE. SO BETTER KEEP A WINDOW OPEN.

THE CAT CAN SEE EVEN IN VERY DIM LIGHT, BECAUSE IT CAN OPEN THE PUPILS OF ITS EYES VERY WIDE TO LET IN WHATEVER LIGHT IS AVAILABLE.

IT USES ITS WHISKERS TO FEEL ITS WAY AROUND.

WHEN YOUR CAT IS SIX MONTHS OLD, IT WILL GO OUT AT NIGHT TO LOOK FOR A MATE.

...AND TOMCATS IN THE AREA WILL RUSH TOWARDS HER.

IF IT'S A FEMALE, SHE'LL MAKE A PECULIAR SOUND (KNOWN AS "CALLING"). THIS SOUND CAN BE HEARD OVER A GREAT DISTANCE...

SOMETIMES TWO OR THREE TOMCATS GATHER TOGETHER AND FIGHT FEROCIOUSLY.

YOUR CAT WILL BE PREGNANT FOR ABOUT 60 DAYS. DURING THIS PERIOD YOU'LL HAVE TO GIVE HER MORE FOOD—ESPECIALLY MILK.

AT THE END OF THE SECOND MONTH, MAKE HER SLEEPING QUARTERS MORE COMFORTABLE. YOUR CAT OF COURSE, WILL RE-ARRANGE THE BED AS SHE WANTS.

AND ONE DAY SHE WILL BECOME VERY UNEASY. IT'S TIME TO DELIVER HER KITTENS. KEEP BOWLS OF MILK AND WATER READY FOR HER. IF SHE NEEDS YOUR HELP, SHE WILL ASK FOR IT. OTHERWISE DON'T INTERFERE IN HER BUSINESS.

WITHIN TWO HOURS SHE'LL BE A MOTHER. MANY PEOPLE THINK THAT THE MOTHER CAT EATS ONE OF HER KITTENS. IT'S NOT TRUE. SHE EATS THE SAC AND PLACENTA OF EACH KITTEN.

THE KITTENS' EYES ARE CLOSED FOR 3 WEEKS. THEIR MOTHER KEEPS THEM WELL FED AND CLEAN BY LICKING THEM.

IF SHE WANTS TO SHIFT, SHE CATCHES HER KITTENS BY A FLAP OF SKIN AT THE BACK OF THE NECK.

AFTER 3 WEEKS, THE KITTENS OPEN THEIR EYES AND BECOME VERY PLAYFUL AND MISCHIEVOUS.

HERE ARE SOME PEDIGREE BREEDS OF CATS:

Black Persian

Chocolate Brown Siamese

Russian Blue

White Persian

Tortoiseshell

Orange Siamese

Kalia
THE CROW

Script:
LUIS

Illustrations:
PRADEEP SATHE

HELLO, THERE!

SSSSH! I'M HIDING FROM BABLOO.

WHAT DID YOU DO?

I ATE A FEW FRUITS FROM HIS CAVE... HEE HEE HEE.

CHAMATAKA, LOOK AT THAT STRANGE BIRD.

IT'S A GOLDEN PLOVER. ITS NEST MUST BE NEARBY, LET'S FOLLOW IT.

I COULD DO WITH A FEW EGGS.

WHY DID IT SUDDENLY SWERVE LIKE THAT?

IT'S TRYING TO LEAD US AWAY FROM ITS NEST.

BUT WE'LL GO STRAIGHT AHEAD... HEE HEE.

YOU'RE SO CLEVER, CHAMATAKA.

A MATTER OF RIGHTS

Story by : Kamini Dinesh
Illustrations : Ram Waeerkar

A SADHU ON HIS DAILY ROUNDS, KNOCKED ON A DOOR.

PRAISE BE TO GOD...

I'M SORRY. I'VE NOTHING TO OFFER.

CHARITY IN THE NAME OF ..

BANG

SHE HAS NO RESPECT FOR SADHUS.

The Chase

Illustrations:
Ram Waeerkar

What Happens Next? Complete this story in 300 words or less and send it to us by 30th August 1983. The best entry will win Rs. 50. *

* Refer to the footnote under the Editor's Note

158

Start a subscription and get a brand new Tinkle issue every fortnight!

Get the latest editions of Tinkle delivered straight to your doorstep!

24 ISSUES

TINKLE MAGAZINE

ANNUAL SUBSCRIPTION

COVER PRICE ₹1200

OFFER PRICE
₹1149

+ Surprise Gift

TINKLE COMBO

ANNUAL SUBSCRIPTION

COVER PRICE ₹3120

OFFER PRICE
₹2149

+ Surprise Gift

24 ISSUES

12 ISSUES

PLEASE ALLOW FOUR TO SIX WEEKS FOR YOUR SUBSCRIPTION TO BEGIN!

OFFER VALID TILL JUNE 30TH 2020

YOUR DETAILS

Full Name: ....   Date of Birth: ☐☐ ☐☐ ☐☐☐☐

Address: ....

City: .... State: ....   Pin Code: ☐☐☐☐☐☐

Phone/Mobile No.: ☐☐☐ ☐☐☐☐☐☐☐☐☐☐

Email: ....

PAYMENT OPTIONS

Parent's Signature

Cheque/DD: ☐☐☐☐☐ drawn in favour of 'ACK MEDIA DIRECT LTD.' on bank ....
.... for amount ....   Dated: ☐☐ / ☐☐ / ☐☐

SEND US YOUR COMPLETED FORM WITH YOUR CHEQUE/DD AT:

ACK Media Direct Ltd., AFL House, 7th Floor, Lok Bharati Complex, Marol-Maroshi Road, Andheri (East), Mumbai 400 059.

MORE WAYS TO SUBSCRIBE: www.amarchitrakatha.com | customerservice@ack-media.com | +91-22-49188881/2